SHOULDER THE SKY

SHOULDER THE SKY

Lesley Choyce

A BOARDWALK BOOK
A MEMBER OF THE DUNDURN GROUP
TORONTO

Editor: Barry Jowett
Copy-Editor: Jennifer Bergeron
Design: Jennifer Scott
Printer: AGMV Marquis

National Library of Canada Cataloguing in Publication Data

Choyce, Lesley, 1951-
    Shoulder the sky / Lesley Choyce.

ISBN 1-55002-415-9

I. Title.

PS8555.H668S47 2002   jC813'.54   C2002-902282-7   PR9199.3.C497S47 2002

2   3   4   5   06   05   04

Canada

THE CANADA COUNCIL | LE CONSEIL DES ARTS
FOR THE ARTS | DU CANADA
SINCE 1957 | DEPUIS 1957

ONTARIO ARTS COUNCIL
CONSEIL DES ARTS DE L'ONTARIO

We acknowledge the support of the **Canada Council for the Arts** and the **Ontario Arts
Council** for our publishing program. We also acknowledge the financial support of the
Government of Canada through the **Book Publishing Industry Development
Program** and **The Association for the Export of Canadian Books**, and the
Government of Ontario through the **Ontario Book Publishers Tax Credit** program.

Printed and bound in Canada.⊕   Printed on recycled paper.   www.dundurn.com

Dundurn Press
8 Market Street
Suite 200
Toronto, Ontario, Canada
M5E 1M6

Dundurn Press
2250 Military Road
Tonawanda NY
U.S.A. 14150

ACKNOWLEDGEMENTS

Special thanks to Julia Swan for early editorial sugges-
tions, Barry Jowett for his enthusiasm and editorial
work, Jennifer Bergeron for copy-editing, and Malcolm
M. Ross for suggesting the title, which is borrowed from
a poem by A.E. Houseman.

This book is dedicated to my friend Luigi Costanzo,
and all other professionals who work with troubled kids.

CHAPTER ONE

I'm sure I had problems even before she died — my mother, that is. After her death, everyone seemed to think that my biggest problem was that I didn't have any problems. Life went on as normal for me without any really obvious changes. That's why I went to see Dave, a psychiatrist unlike any other shrink around. Unconventional is probably the word that fits.

Dave encouraged me to write my story, and now that it's done, I don't mind that you are reading this. I originally meant to show only Dave and no one else, but then I figured, what the heck. So, if you are reading this now, I don't feel it's like an invasion of privacy or anything.

There's probably not going to be much here that is all that secret. All you will find out is what happened, what I really thought, what I felt, and what I imagined. I better admit up front, though, that I had holes in my memory.

Like holes in socks or black holes in deep space. Like missing pages from a book or scenes snipped out of a movie.

Also, I should tell you that, in a sense, there were three versions of me. There was the regular, not-too-interesting private me: Martin Emerson. Then there was the enigmatic public persona of me that was created for the Internet at Emerso.com. Even though it ends in com, I never sold stuff. The site was very successful. I wrote about anything that went through my head. I also gave advice for free to anyone who wanted to hear what I had to say. People in the real world knew me as Martin Emerson. On the web, I somehow evolved into Emerso. People who visited my site didn't know I was only sixteen years old. They believed I was older and smarter than I really was. More on that later.

Then there was the no-name Martin, Martin number three. This version couldn't remember parts of the past and sometimes couldn't remember where he was the night before. I didn't have too many clues about exactly who he was or what he was up to. Not until we left for Alaska.

Anyway, Dave always wanted me to write something about my mother and my father, so I'll start there. If I get going about website stuff again, tell me to shut up.

My mother was creative. She made paintings of places that looked completely different from where we lived.

My father thought they looked like Asia, but I always thought they were alien landscapes: the deserts of Mars, maybe, or swirling gassy places on Jupiter. But my father was pretty sure it was Asia. My sister, Lilly, always said she hated my mother's paintings. Until my mother died, that is, and then Lilly put many of the paintings in her room — the ones that were finished. The unfinished ones, my father tried to complete, and that didn't turn out well at all.

My mother once told me that painting is just another way of keeping a diary. This didn't help explain the alien/Asian landscape paintings, but maybe it fits in with Dave's idea about me keeping a journal.

For a long time after my mom's death I called my father the Invisible Man. Sometimes you could see him when he moved through rooms or went out the door. You could see him clearly when he was behind the wheel of the van, backing too quickly out the driveway. But most of the time he was invisible. Or not there at all.

My very first posting on Emerso.com went like this.

http://www.Emerso.com

Welcome to my website. This website is designed to improve the world, and if you aren't interested in that you should probably go to another site. That's perfectly fine with me. I will update it when I have the time. If you found this at all, it is probably because you were looking for something else. My friend the Egg Man taught me how to mess with search engines. He is really good if you ever want the world to go to your website. I think he charges money now but he did it for me for free — as they say, that's what friends are for.

The Egg Man taught me how to do this: let's say you want to find out about how zippers work, or if coffee can kill you, or you want to know more about Britney Spears' tonsillectomy (or maybe it's Madonna), or, say, *Star Wars* toys. You type in "Madonna" or "*Star Wars* toys" and you end up at Emerso.com.

I just wanted to be up front about how you got here. You can leave any time you like but if you stick around you may learn something. I've got a few things figured out and I'm figuring out more every day. I hope to deal with the really difficult issues, like what is the meaning of life, and why do people die, but I will also be discussing less important things like brand names, politics, coffee, revenge, teachers, chewing gum, and whether or not God exists. I'm not selling anything on this website so you don't have to have your credit card handy.

Also, my friend the Egg Man taught me how to make sure that my identity remains a secret. If you try to trace the origin of the site, you'll hit a dead end. It's not that I'm famous or doing anything illegal. I just want my privacy. We all deserve our privacy. That's one of the rules here at Emerso.com. It's my only rule so far, but I'll probably come up with a few others as things develop.

So far there are seven choices to click on if you want to explore Emerso further:

1. Meaning of Life (under construction).
2. Stuff That May or May Not Be Important.
3. Junk.
4. Opinions.
5. Advice.
6. Art.
7. The Universe.

If you are wasting time like this, just goofing around on the Internet and still at my site, it's possible that your life is, well, not all that exciting. No offence. Just a candid observation. Some of what I have to offer may or may not help, but one thing I am sure of is that you have a limited time here on earth, so you need to get on with something or other — just about anything, as long as it doesn't hurt people or small animals.

Emerso

CHAPTER TWO

Not long after our mom died, I tried to talk to my sister, Lilly, but she didn't want to talk about it. My mother had an illness that lasted about four years. It was not cancer but it might as well have been. She had treatment and got better and then got worse and we all did very poorly in dealing with it and with her.

My father was trying, but he was already turning invisible and that didn't help. Lilly was rebellious at the time. She had even changed her name to Lilith for a while when she discovered that Lilith, in Jewish folklore, was a vampire-like killer and nocturnal female demon. Older than me, she was experimenting with drugs and dying her hair and she kept finding some new part of her body to pierce. She was angry almost all the time, which seemed all wrong to me but, as Dave would say, she was probably venting her anger about our mother dying. Unfortunately, she was mostly angry with our mother for being so sick, and that wasn't Mom's fault.

Lilly stayed out really late, and once she got into trouble with the police at an all-night rave. That surprised me because she always told me she hated rave music. Lilly and I could never talk to each other about my mother's condition when Mom was alive. None of us were big talkers in my family. That's why Dave thought that writing would be a good way for me to "open up." Dave didn't know about my website back then.

My mother — and I want to use her first name here — Claire — was brave about the fact that she was slipping downhill. Her paintings of the alien landscapes got much better. She tried to open up more about herself and she tried to pull the family together even as it was falling apart. My mother, I now believe, was like the sun — bright and cheery and a great warm gravity anchor that held all of us little planets in orbit. When she died, we all went spinning off into the void.

But the odd thing was that, to everyone around us, we seemed like we were handling it well. We acted as if nothing particularly important had happened. Lilly kept sulking and piercing and sometimes smoking. She went through a string of truly repulsive boyfriends, even one who was the lead singer in a band called Repuke.

My father made hasty, furtive appearances around home, slipping in and out of the bathroom, in and out of the kitchen, holed up watching hockey on TV in the bedroom, and slipping out to his van in the morning to go to work just as I was waking up — and it didn't seem to matter what time I woke up.

It was a month after Claire had died that my math teacher — the HMMWMT (heavy metal mud wrestling math teacher) took me aside and said, "Martin, you have a serious problem. I think you are too normal and it's not normal to be normal after you've had a trauma in your life."

Mr. Miller, HMMWMT (who only mud wrestled at bars on weekends after his professional career as a world champion wrestler had ended), was one of the few people in the school kids listened to. He had once played a really nasty lead guitar in a heavy metal band called Gangrene, and they sold a lot of CDs before he retired from the road and took up teaching math. He still had a small ponytail even though he was kind of bald up top. And once every week Mr. Miller would bring in his Fender guitar and Marshall amp and try to explain algebra using some screeching distortion riffs that would bring the principal banging on the door. The principal never actually walked in to say anything, because nobody messed with the HMMWMT. But if Mr. Miller saw his boss peering in through the little window in the door, he'd crank the amp back to five instead of ten.

It was the HMMWMT who told me I should go see a "professional" about my problem. He explained that my kind of "personal dilemma" needed something more than that wimp, Egan, our guidance counsellor, could offer. When Mr. Miller takes you aside, you listen, so I knew I had to take the advice. He recommended his old friend Dave, who had once been a roadie for Meatloaf before taking up psychiatry. And the rest, as they say, is history. Or my story, at least.

CHAPTER THREE

Dave and Mr. Miller agreed that I should seek out some form of rebellion to release my anger. I still wasn't sure I had anger. Hurt and disappointment, however, were present and deeply buried in the suitcase of my mind. I suppose I had learned from my father — or somehow inherited his genetic code — to keep things bottled up. We were not moaners, complainers, whiners, or wimps in the Emerson household, and I had descended, apparently, from very stoic apes, followed by a genealogical string of New England workaholics who faced life's adversities with coping mechanisms that required no tears.

I asked Lilly to take me somewhere to have my nose or my ear pierced but I chickened out when I saw the young woman — not much older than Lilly — who was about to do the job. She claimed to be a professional, but

I could tell that she had been drinking. I came home without a puncture or laceration and so I failed to get my anger out by means of primitive body defacement.

Every day at noon, however, I had watched the teenaged smokers from my school march in a purposeful but ragged procession towards the woods, where they would smoke away lunch hour instead of sitting in the cafeteria with the rest of us eating cafeteria food or scarfing down homemade mock chicken sandwiches. I had a kind of breakthrough one day there in the cafeteria, unwrapping a sandwich I had packed that morning: bologna with relish, pickles, mustard, and salsa. The sandwich reminded me, with the force of a hurricane ripping the roof off a Florida condominium, how much I missed my mother's vegetarian sandwiches.

My mother had been a vegetarian, although she could never fully explain why. She wasn't an animal rights person or a gung-ho health nut. But she had met a woman who claimed to be a shaman, and the shaman (who sold real estate for a living) told her to cut down on the meat her family was eating. My father, not wanting to cause an argument, went along with it, even though he was a great lover of nearly raw steaks consumed on family pilgrimages to Ponderosa.

The sandwiches my mother created for me were fashioned from homemade brown bread, lentils, sprouts, tofu, three kinds of pickles, salsa, and relish. The other kids all had great pity for me, but I had eaten the sand-wiches dutifully.

Until my mother was too sick to make them. Then I was on my own with bologna or mock chick-en, but I could never face tofu in the morning. And what was left of my family had regressed to white sliced bread as well.

So I was eating lunch with the Egg Man — my friend Darrell — who had his usual egg salad sandwich (but that was not why he was called the Egg Man), and studying the various varieties of pickles as they fell from my sandwich. The cafeteria was loud and making my ears ring. Dave and Heavy Metal Math were still occasionally hounding me about my normality, and I had my own pri-vate disappointments with the failed piercing. The Egg Man was going on and on about how to fool search engines into sending people to his site — which was then an odd combination of images of movie stars from the fifties in bathing suits, reposted tirades against marijuana, sound bites from NASA, and his own personal rants against cellphones. Through the window I could see the parade of smokers heading to the woods. The guys were all stoop-shouldered and the girls wore short skirts and multilevel shoes that seemed completely wrong for tromping into the semi-wilderness. But they looked deliberate and determined — and I decided I wanted to be one of them.

School and smoking have never had an easy relationship, as far as I can tell. Bathroom smoking was always a covert activity where someone eventually got caught and got into trouble. Kids used to be able to smoke outside of some schools — right on the grounds — but non-smoking perimeters kept spiralling outward from school buildings. Fortunately, as long as you didn't live in a big city, there always seemed to be some nearby woods to sneak off into for a smoke.

The principal knew who smoked where at our school. So did the guidance counsellor, Mr. Egan. Heck, all the teachers knew. Lectures had been delivered in hallways more than a few times. Once, the HMMWMT walked out at noon hour to try to convince the smokers that they were ruining their lungs, shortening their lives, and even promoting possible future sexual incapacity. But they wouldn't listen even to him. And if you couldn't be persuaded by the HMMWMT, no one was going to change your mind.

But remember, Dave and Heavy Metal had told me I needed some kind of rebellion, and today was my day. I left the Egg Man to dream on about ways to fool the new search engines and I went to the woods to smoke.

They all stared at me at first. Some of the guys laughed but took elbows in the ribs from girls who knew about the death of my mother. Intuitively, they knew why I was there. Bill, a guy I'd known since elementary school, shook a cigarette out of a pack and handed it to one of the girls. I was a little surprised to see Scott Rutledge there. Scott must have arrived by his own alternate, less conspicuous route. That's because Scott was the one kid in school that everyone admired. Teachers liked him. Girls adored him. He could clown with the hooligans but he was also kind to the geeks.

It was Scott who flipped a cigarette my way. A lighter flared, and I leaned and sucked at my very first tug of smoke. Everyone waited for me to cough, but I did not. Only a wisp of tobacco and nicotine had passed my lips and descended into my lungs. But I exhaled with enthusiasm and took a second drag. People nodded and approved. I felt like I had been accepted into a sacred religious cult.

The girls all tried to look sexy (or were sexy, depending on who it was) and the guys all looked like actors who played the roles of young thugs in made-for-TV movies. I didn't try too hard to look cool because I knew I couldn't pull it off.

The conversation was mostly about how ugly all the teachers were and how messed up the school was. There was universal agreement about those two subjects. I offered no opinions but was halfway though my second cigarette when the bell rang. Amazingly, the thugs and chicks (the guys actually got away with calling girls "chicks" in this primordial world of green leaves and ritual smoke) all dropped their butts, ground them into the rich forest soil with heavy heels, and turned towards the school. Scott nodded at me and headed off for his circuitous path back to class.

Somebody slapped me on the back. "Back to the hellhole," Bill said.

"What it is," someone else said.

A couple of girls pulled out mirrors and lipstick as they walked. For the first time in my life, I was viewed as being at least semi-cool by the other kids in the cafeteria as I walked back into the school with the smokers. And I felt a kind of pride.

My mother would have been appalled if she could have known. It had been a rapid descent from tofu and brown bread to this tobacco wasteland. My father would simply not have believed I smoked, even if I lit up in the living room and inhaled a pack of Marlboros, puffing smoke in his face with every lungful. The truth is that I didn't like the smoking part, but I felt pretty good about the camaraderie. I wished that non-smokers could sneak off into the woods to stand around and not smoke and that this would somehow be considered dangerous and even sexy. But the world is a funny place, eh, and things don't always work out the way you want them to.

And you'll be disappointed to learn that by the time I got back to math class, where Heavy Metal was tuning up his Fender for geometry, I felt let down that smoking had not made me feel angrier about anything. I knew I was still holding it all back, a great dam against some flood that Dave explained should come some day, a flood I needed to be prepared for. But it wasn't today. My mother was still gone from the world and I had somehow accepted this fact with only a lingering twinge of self-pity. I was still acting way too normal for my own good.

CHAPTER FOUR

When I told Dave about the smoking, he looked concerned at first but then cleared his throat and said, "I think this is actually a good thing. A few more bad habits and we'll have you cured."

I knew that Dave was not like conventional shrinks. He said he tried to come up with creative approaches to problems, approaches that might seem totally whacked to some. But he was confident that he was on the right track with me.

"What exactly is it you're trying to cure me of," I asked, "aside from my problem of being so normal, or at least appearing to be normal?"

"Sheesh," Dave said. "Maybe cure is the wrong word. I'm just trying to help. It has to do with your mother, remember. You must miss her a lot."

"I do. Every minute of the day."

"That's good."

"It is?"

"You loved her?"

"Of course; she was my mother. Did you love your mother?"

"I still do."

"She's alive?"

"Yes. Nearly eighty. She still tells me I need a haircut every time I see her."

"You do need a haircut. For an old guy, you look a little flaky with that shaggy mop and those sideburns."

"You think I should look normal?"

"No. Maybe not."

"Meanwhile, back at the ranch…" he said, which was Dave's way of trying to get back on subject — this issue of me and the fact I'd been acting so seemingly normal, which seemed to upset everyone so much. "How do you feel about this smoking thing?"

So we did that one long and hard. Maybe I was acting out my anger and my hurt. That was the theory. Dave didn't have to give me a lecture about the fact that my smoking career should be short. From the start, I knew I couldn't commit myself to the smoking lifestyle. I was pretty sure it wasn't worth lung cancer and sexual dysfunction.

My only true commitment to the smoking world was love of the foray into the woods at noon hour and then right after school, a quick couple of puffs with the gang at the designated spot near the bus garage followed by running for the bus with nicotine breath. Sometimes it was me keeping pace with Scott Rutledge, which must have raised a few eyebrows at the mingling of such strange companions.

I gave smoking a full two weeks of my life. It was a five-days-a-week thing. No weekends. What was the point if I was not with my squint-eyed smoky tribe? So it was ten days, four smokes a day. Mostly I bummed cigarettes, but nobody would have put up with that for much longer.

I tried to tell my father that I started smoking. He was watching golf on TV. During golf my father was visible but pretty much comatose. It wasn't from drinking or anything. It was his own special narcotic state of half sleep/half golf. He didn't even like golf but he liked the hue of the greens, the hushed crowds, and the well-appointed golfers selecting woods or irons. It was another world for him. My father had no bad habits that I knew of, and the Saturday afternoon TV golf/semi-sleep seemed to be enough to transport him from the real world into a dimension akin to a heroin high. I'm just guessing but I think there's truth in it.

"I've started smoking," I told him. He was lost on the seventh green somewhere outside Atlanta.

"That's not a good idea," he said, drifting, I think, somewhere above the Georgian treetops.

"No kidding."

"You really are?"

"Yep."

"I'll be darned."

That was it. I don't think he believed me. It just wasn't the sort of thing his son Martin would do.

Opinions

Trees deserve more respect and credit than we give them. Nobody should be allowed to cut down a tree, any tree, without being charged a fee or a tax or something that would then go to health care for poor people. The tree tax would have to be passed on to consumers and that way we'd know a tree had been sacrificed every time we bought something that was part tree.

I was thinking about trees because of the days spent in the woods with the smokers. In the end, I liked the trees better than the puff fiends. Smoking had been part of my quest for healing. I wanted to damage myself somehow, Dave had suggested. But I think that was just the shrink in him talking. I wanted communion with someone and the smokers took me in — or out to the woods, at least.

But I had to give up on being part of that squint-eyed but oh-so-cool squad. My breath smelled bad — my teachers said so — but that's not why I gave up on smoking. I could have taken that flack. It was the smokers' conversation that did me in. The complaints about teachers and homework. How creepy the principal was. Older siblings who were getting in trouble with the law over petty crimes and automobile offences.

I'd try to initiate new subjects. I started pointing out different trees one day. "This old oak here must be over a hundred years old."

The girls looked at me like I'd arrived from Jupiter. Finster and Hubbards, both older and more threatening than the other guys, looked somehow offended. "How do you know?" Finster asked in an intimidating manner.

"Yeah," Hubbards asked, "what are you, like some bloody tree expert?"

I could tell they weren't interested in my thoughts on the maples, oaks, gums, birches, poplars, or any of the shrubby undergrowth. Instead, the conversation turned, as it always did, back to cigarettes. Which was the subject that drove me from the fold.

"I really could have used a cigarette during that test in math," Cindy said.

"I nearly died for a smoke towards the end of history. It was like so boring."

"I don't think it's fair we can't smoke in class," Scott Rutledge added, fine-tuning his agenda for the race for class president.

"God this tastes good," Finster said, dragging smoke into his lungs.

"Do you believe they're raising the price of a pack of smokes again?" Hubbards asked the elms.

"I smoked two whole packs on Sunday," somebody else confessed with pride. "My folks were gone."

Etcetera.

And so my smoking career ended of its own accord. Whatever it was supposed to do for me, it wasn't working. It didn't make me angry or release my emotions. I wasn't edgy and nervous with chips on my shoulder like the rest of the gang, and I think eventually they would have simply told me to stop hanging out with them. The simple comment about the age of the tree had set off a lot of mistrust. Finster and Hubbards were beginning to think I was some kind of mole or snitch. So I faded from their lives as quickly as I had entered.

And then I woke up one night soon after, remembering something.

I was twelve and my mother and I were sitting in the kitchen. She was peeling potatoes, and I liked watching her do this — graceful, artistic, long spirals of potato skin being released from the spud, revealing a cold white flesh beneath. Out of the blue, she said, "You know, I smoked one cigarette in my entire life."

"You did?"

"I was about your age. An older boy gave it to me. I didn't smoke it then but took it home and lit it up behind the house. I was all alone. I sipped at the smoke. I didn't haul it in like most amateurs do. I never coughed. I liked it. It made me feel important. There was no filter. I smoked it down until it burned my fingers. And then it was over. I loved every minute of it. I especially liked the way that the world looked through the smoke that was right in front of my face."

She saw the stunned look on *my* face. She was scaring me because she was revealing something of herself that seemed very private.

"That's why I never touched another one. Don't you ever start, okay?"

The final parental caution seemed like it was tagged on as an afterthought. Obligatory. She wasn't really trying to give me a lecture. Remembering that one-sided conversation brought her back to me for a brief moment.

"Claude Monet," she had said, "was a French painter who said that he did not paint the object but the space between the viewer and the object. That was where the smoke took me."

And that was part of what was happening in her paintings, I soon realized. Whether it was Asia or other worlds, the air was thick with diffused colours. It was a beautiful distant place my mother went to when she painted. But I don't think any of us in the family ever went there with her. The paintings themselves had created barriers, or maybe we had created them ourselves.

I was beginning to wish I had asked my mother more questions when she was alive.

CHAPTER FIVE

Advice

My advice to you today is to shut off your computer. Maybe there are two kinds of people: those who live life and those who are just an audience. We're all becoming lazy and stupid because of our machines. Get out of the house and do anything that does not involve electricity. You don't want to hear this, but it needs to be said.

Dave said that Lilly was right on track with her anger. "She is working it out," he told me. But Lilly was rebellious and angry before my mother got sick, while she was sick, and now Lilly was still angry. She had pierced her nose recently, which would make anyone cranky, I would think. But she was proud of it. And she shaved off all the hair in her eyebrows. I don't know why a person would do that, but she must have felt it was important. "It's a statement," she told me. Whatever that means.

Lilly had given up smoking herself, but she still stayed out late with people who seemed odious to me. Her "friend" Jake had bleached blond hair and wore a black leather jacket with little metal things stamped into it. Apparently, people, including Lilly, thought Jake was really something. But I wasn't impressed. He always had a look on his face like he had just done something really nasty and felt good about it. I'm sure he had been working on that look for many years. Lilly thought he was "deep."

If you asked him what he'd been up to he always answered, "Not much." In that regard, I think he had some sincerity.

Jake, along with the others, encouraged Lilly to stay out too late doing "not much," but so far it hadn't seemed to do her much harm. I think hers was a crowd that tried to be nasty, cruel, and even hurtful — but they couldn't quite pull it off. So they wandered around in some cynical limbo world of what someone once called "quiet desperation."

I explained this all to Dave and he said that this was a "common malady" of many young people today. (Not like when he was growing up and young people knew exactly why they were angry and who they were angry at.) Anger, even frustrated anger, Dave would explain, is better than apathy. Dave was a real stickler when it came to apathy. He ranted about apathy. Just to get his goat, I told him I was apathetic about apathy. He almost lost his cookies until he realized I was messing with his head.

"Good one, dude," he said, finally taking a breath. "Physician heal thyself. Right on." Then he tightened the rubber band on his little ponytail and we continued talking about me and my problem of acting so normal.

Disappointment with my short-lived smoking career sent me back to a traditional cafeteria lunch with Darrell. Darrell was a loner like me, and when two loners go separate paths, well, you just have two individual loners instead of two loners who hang out together.

"I felt forsaken," Darrell said. I know that doesn't sound like anything a kid would say, but neither Darrell nor I have ever spoken in the same manner as our contemporaries. This is why sometimes we were referred to as "intellectual snot" — or "snots" if we were being referred to in the plural.

"It was just an experiment," I said.

Darrell understood all about experiments. "How'd it turn out?"

"I had high expectations, but it didn't make orbit."

"Been there, done that. Got the T-shirt for it."

We liked to mix idioms. In fact, we liked the word "idiom" a lot and fantasized starting a band called the Idiom Idiots, just Darrell and me and about a hundred thousand dollars worth of computerized music and sound gear.

While I'd been trying to learn how to smoke, Darrell had been up to his own experiments. I noticed he was wolfing down a tuna sandwich: whole wheat, heavy mayonnaise, sliced pickles protruding from the edges. "Martino, I thought long and hard about your alliance with coffin nails and came to the conclusion that I too need some way to break out of this shell I've created for myself."

Heck, we were both a couple of geeks but, I had always thought, well-adjusted geeks, in a world that was soon to be ruled by geeks like us: non-smokers, smarter than we let on, not particularly attractive to girls or women, young men who handed in acceptable homework assignments and went to bed early.

Darrell offered me half of his tuna sandwich. His mother always cut it in half to form two rectangles. My own mother never failed to cut corner to corner, creating two perfect triangles. If she made tuna fish, she would always put fresh dill or fennel in it. I accepted the tuna fish and Darrell brushed his hands theatrically, leaned over, and pulled a dozen eggs out of his book bag. He placed the egg container in front of him and, like he was opening some box of precious jewels, he lifted the lid.

"I've come to the conclusion I was leading a much too sheltered life. As you know, I studied the Klingon dictionary and became somewhat proficient in the language. But it wasn't until I found myself staying up late conversing on a chat room in Klingon with people all over the planet — for up to two hours at a time — that I realized I needed to get out of the house and do something a bit more ambitious with my life."

"Now you're raising chickens?"

"No."

"Ukrainian egg decorating?"

"Get serious."

"I give. What are you doing with the eggs?"

"Revenge," was Darrell's one word answer.

CHAPTER SIX

☁ ☁ ☁

Stuff That May or May Not Be Important

Human kind has never perfected alternatives to war, but there must ultimately be alternatives. Simple co-operation between people and countries is probably not sexy enough. Deep inside the grey matter of our brains, they say, we are still basically lizards. If you dig further, we are probably just amoebas, but we don't think like amoebas anymore (the exception being the writers and producers of most TV sitcoms).

Our reptilian brains seize on territorial notions, convincing our weaker rational brains that we have legitimate reasons for organized violence, and we become aggravated and aggressive.

It is my contention that we are not evolving into anything more advanced than we now are — at least our brains are not evolving. We may end up without a little toe or a thumb but we will still have urges to do harm and to wage war.

Since evolution will not save us from ourselves — in fact, it may make us more aggressive — we must seek alternatives.

Darrell really didn't have that many enemies. He was more enamoured with the idea of revenge than with any Edgar Allan Poetic obsession to do harm to those he hated.

Holding up a brown egg in front of the intergalactic screen saver on his computer, he said, "Behold, the perfect creative weapon."

"Some would see it as a food source."

"That troubled me at first. I was buying at the supermarket and wondering if there were alternatives. I asked the guy working the aisles what they do with old eggs."

"Old eggs?"

"Ones that have been in the store too long. Unsold eggs. They must go somewhere. It turns out there's a company that buys them — dirt cheap. I tracked it down and found the place. Went there on the bus. They use old eggs to cook up and then freeze dry or something. I was afraid to ask too much. But I asked the guy if I could buy some old eggs from him. I said I was doing experiments. Research. Now I have a guilt-free source of cheap eggs."

On my own, I would never have achieved the same drive and passion for focused or even random egg violence that Darrell had, but I was still on my quest for an emotional outlet and here was an opportunity not to be passed up. It was a vice far more addicting than tobacco, and we both quickly passed from focused acts of egg revenge to random acts of egg aggression.

Darrell was my tutor. At first we were pretty adolescent about it all. Eggs placed on the chairs of less favoured teachers. Eggs placed on fluorescent light fixtures in classrooms, hair-triggered on their perch, sure to drop if anyone so much as slammed a door. A more subtle approach to in-school egg activity was a simple egg with a pin hole or two placed in the back of a teacher's desk drawer or perhaps in an unlucky locker. Eventually the egg would rot and the smell would be sulfuric, odoriferous, and downright diabolic. Eggs rolled down the aisles of buses to be squashed by the feet of third graders.

When the work crew came to begin to clear the woods behind the school for a new shopping mall, we smeared eggs on the windshields of trucks and dozers. Later we would learn that smearing cheese on car windows was another way to wreak havoc with the so-called civilized world.

We never threw eggs at people. We had our limits. We did pitch a couple dozen eggs at cigarette billboards and the signs of a few wrong-headed hopeful candidates in an upcoming election.

The Egg Man and I kept our identities nicely concealed. The school authorities were well aware of the "egg problem." There had been small editorials railing against us in the local paper. Rotten eggs were turning up all over the school. There was talk of having to close the school for fear of harmful health effects.

And so Darrell and I decided one day, walking home from school, that our egg careers were over. We had become egg junkies and enjoyed the thrill of revenge on a world gone mad, but it had gone far enough.

As mysteriously as the egg raids began, they stopped, except for a smattering of copycat egg vandals who were quickly caught, and then punished by their humiliated parents.

Dave knew what we had been up to but he said he had sworn some oath that he could never rat on one of his clients. I think he got some kind of second-hand satisfaction from our insanely juvenile deeds. But he was disappointed when I told him that I did it all without malice. As my mother would have said, "It was just a phase I had to go through."

My father didn't know that I was the subject of the anti-egg vandal editorials, and Lilly didn't care. She had her own stash of anger. She had garnered a monopoly on all the anger available in our family.

I went back to being even more normal than I'd been before. I slept well at night and dreamed of flying. When I woke in the morning I was neither happy nor sad to see the new day. Raining or sunshine, it all pretty much meant the same to me. Darrell went back to trying to hack into Microsoft. We communed at lunch over the triviality of life. I did well in school. I missed the feel of a perfectly formed egg fitted into the palm of my hand and that was about it.

CHAPTER SEVEN

Stuff That May or May Not Be Important

I'm pretty sure there are intelligent alien beings living among us. They live on another plane of existence, though, and we can't really detect them except with our minds. They are responsible for much of the unexplainable stuff that goes on out there. Lost socks, for example. Unlike our expectations, the invisible aliens are not highly intelligent. Just because you live on another plane of existence doesn't mean you are ultra-smart.

They are, however, better at bridging the barrier between our physical world and their world. They can pick up our television broadcasts, and this has convinced them not to invent their own version of TV. Their best scientists, however, after decades of research, devised a method for stealing socks from our world.

That's where your socks go — one at a time, never by twos. They have been unable to develop a means to transport two socks at a time to their world. If ever someone comes up with an accidental match, those socks are highly prized possessions in the other world.

It is not a mirror universe or anything like that. There is no version of "you" there. The inhabitants are not happier or sadder than us. They have their own version of ice cream and they have holidays — one even commemorating the first time a sock was ever transported across the void to their world. They know the name of the man in our world who lost the very first human sock to them. And that man is somewhat famous in a nebulous sort of way over there.

Much of what we do is inexplicable to them. Much of what they do is inexplicable to us. Some day we will devise a way to communicate with them, but we may save them a lot of grief if we don't. Humans have a way of screwing up "first contact" really badly. Which is why all truly intelligent aliens — amongst us or out in space — try to keep their distance and maintain a low profile.

Not long after the egg phase, I got the idea in my head that I should commit acts of random generosity. I should do good deeds. If possible, I should do them without anyone knowing that I was doing them. My "victims" would be people who were down and out, especially losers.

I made the mistake of discussing this with my sister while her friend Jake was over.

"You want to do what?" Jake asked, tugging at his earring.

"I told you my brother was weird," Lilly said.

"We live in a very predictable world where people tend to look out for number one. I want to mess with that."

"But why would you want to do something nice for other people?" Jake asked. "Everything sucks. It's a well-known fact. Life is about trying to get away with stuff. That's why we are here. It's like a game that has certain rules. You're messing with the rules."

"I know. That's the point."

Lilly tried to defend me. "He's seeing a shrink."

"His name is Dave," I added.

"Dave told my kid brother he should smoke."

"He's a wise man," Jake said approvingly.

I hung my head, feeling a certain amount of shame. "It didn't work out. I just wasn't a smoker."

"You have to give it time," Jake said. I could tell he genuinely felt sorry for me and my failure at smoking.

So it was Saturday and I was trying to figure a way to commit acts of random goodness. I thought of phoning Darrell to come along but I was not sure he was ready for this. It might not work out at all, so I figured I would go it alone for a while. Where to begin?

All I could think of was mowing lawns. Two doors down lived Mr. Sheldon. Gus Sheldon. He was downsized when one bank bought another bank. He ran into some personal slippage after that. Wife left him to work in a casino in Las Vegas. Then Gus settled into a job doing people's taxes at H&R Block, but he started drinking on the job. Then came a job working nights at a Quick-Way. He drank there, too. Now he just drank at home and slept in late.

So I mowed his lawn with our mower and he woke up around noon to see that someone had cut his grass while he slept in. Later, I would learn that he thought he did it himself while he was tanked and couldn't remember. Afraid that he might do it again and maybe cut off his toes or something, he put his lawnmower out for the trash. He wasn't interested in lawn care anymore anyway.

I know my mother would have liked the random kindness business. She used to give her paintings to sick friends until she discovered that giving away homemade pies worked better. Even if they didn't eat it, people cheered up when my Mom delivered a pie. Not everybody "got" my mother's paintings. She was pretty far out there.

Because of my mother and the pies, I decided not to give up. There were other acts of random kindness. I sent anonymous compliments to people by e-mail. Darrell showed me how to do this so no one would know it was me. I told ugly girls they were pretty. I told losers they were admired. I would always be very specific, nothing generic.

I tried in vain to do some nice things for people at the mall, but somehow it just didn't feel right there. I told one of my classmates, Julie, that the shoes she was about to buy in one store were actually ten dollars cheaper in another store. She just gave me a dirty look.

I opened the glass mall door for a woman carrying two heavy bags, but she walked through without acknowledging me at all. I even cleaned up the scraps of paper on the floor around the money machine. That was what brought the security guard.

"What do you think you're doing?" the uniformed guy asked. You could tell he'd watched a few too many cop movies.

"Tidying up," I answered.

"There's no loitering allowed in the mall."

"I understand the need for rules," I said.

"Good. Then you'll understand why I have to ask you to leave."

"No problem."

I was going to offer to buy him a cup of coffee but I'd lost confidence.

I told Lilly about my efforts.

"How do you get into this stuff?" she asked. "You're such a dork."

Then she went into one of her well-rehearsed acts of exasperation for an audience that wasn't even there. "My brother is such a dork," she said to herself in the mirror. Lilly often talked to herself in the mirror when she needed to express an important thought. "He is like so not-there."

I didn't take any of it personally. I waited for her to turn around.

"Nice outfit."

"This old thing? I hate it."

"It looks good on you."

"Oh pa-lease."

"What are we going to do about Dad?" I asked, changing the subject.

"What is there to do? He's invisible. Not on the radar at all. He is who he wants to be. Why should we intrude on his coping mechanism?"

"Maybe he shouldn't be invisible."

"Martin, you're the one with the wise-ass shrink. What would he say?" she asked.

"He'd say that Dad has to get mad at something."

"Great. Then he'd start yelling at us like he used to."

"He didn't yell that much."

"Not at you. You're such a dork. You never got into trouble."

"I tried."

"No one thinks like you do, Martin. You're on your own little planetoid. The Moon of Martin."

"It's who I am."

"Martin. Face it. We have a weird family. All families are weird as soon as you get to know them. We're no different."

"Except that we lost Mom."

"Why did you have to bring that up?"

"Sorry."

I turned to leave.

"Come back here," she said. Suddenly my sister was giving me a big hug. She was crying but pretending not to be. "Martin from the Moon. My little brother."

Quote of the Day

"I'll be damned if I'll let any old nebula get in our way."

Captain Katherine Janeway,
Star Trek: Voyager

CHAPTER EIGHT

Meaning of Life

For those who need something new to agonize about: some scientists occasionally worry that something really catastrophic will happen if all of the planets line up on the same side of the sun. You know, they're all spinning around in their own orbits and there's a kind of balance. But about once every thousand years, say, they end up on the same side of the solar system and all in a straight line. Something weird could happen.

The great thing about getting serious about worrying about catastrophes that are of a solar system proportion is that you can stop fussing with dumb little worries that clutter up your life. Suppose the scientists say that next Thursday all the planets will line up on the same side of the solar system and we might experience earthquakes, increased solar radiation, firestorms, and waves that are two hundred feet high crashing against the continent.

This all sounds pretty wicked and you decide that the problem you have with your chequing account or those new shoes you can't afford or the fact that you haven't changed the oil in your car for several years — well, they all seem kind of trivial.

If you are a kid in school and believe the world will be destroyed next Thursday, the odds are you will stop doing your homework. You won't give a rat's ass about the math test next Friday because it will all be smoke and rubble by then.

So you maximize the amount of happiness you can cram in between now and next Thursday. You're convinced there is nothing you can do to save yourself, your family, or the pet turtle you named Will Smith.

The conclusion here is that, for the right people, catastrophes, or even belief in catastrophes, can be a great way to improve your life. If the catastrophe does not happen, you have to backpeddle a little and cope with the mess of things not done until the next predicted catastrophe comes along. But you will have created a grace period in which you will have stopped fussing and allowed yourself to be the happy human you are capable of being. Keep well informed through the media about potential sunspots, meteor showers, volcanic activity, odd migration patterns of birds, and threats from intelligent deep-sea creatures.

"What the heck is going on? I can't find my car keys. Does anybody know what happened to my car keys?"

I had not been awakened by the sound of my father's voice in a long time. Invisible and silent had been his style. It was good to hear his voice. I climbed out of bed and stumbled down the stairs.

"Martin, do you know where my keys are?"

"I'll help you find them." Somehow, I always knew where the lost car keys were.

"I always keep them hanging up here by the refrigerator. Always."

"I know. Did you have any breakfast?" Sometimes I worry that my father is not taking care of himself.

"I don't have time. I've got a meeting with Product Development in twenty minutes. And I can't find my darn keys."

Ever since my mother died, my father stopped using swear words. When she was alive, he was a bit foul-mouthed for a father. He was a nice guy, don't get me wrong, just a big fan of four-letter words. Now he only used "heck" and "darn" and other replacement words — like "schist" — that came close to sounding like the real things. This was a kind of tribute to her.

I saw the keys to the van. "Here, Dad. They're here by the toaster." I knew they were there even before I looked. Or rather, the other Martin, Martin number three, knew. And that made me feel a little spooked.

But my dad was happy. "Thanks, Martin. You saved the day."

He almost gave me eye contact but he turned quickly. "Remind me to get an extra set of keys made for the van." He was doing that father rushing around bit, slurping coffee from a cup, spilling it, and getting his arm stuck in the sleeve of his suit jacket.

He was just about out the door when he turned. "Martin?"

"Yeah?"

He looked at his watch. "Later."

The door closed.

The van, which my father now started up and backed out of the driveway, was a family decision. Back before we knew my mother was sick, there was this plan to drive it all over North America — on weekends and during the three weeks my father had off in the summer. Lilly was not in favour of the plan unless Jake could come along. "When hell freezes over," my father used to say. My father and Jake never got along.

My mother had maps of all the states and provinces. She really wanted to go to Alaska. She said she would do all the driving. I wished I were old enough to do some of the driving. I wanted to drive my family to Alaska — but not with Jake along.

Every time I got into the van now, I thought of my mother driving us to Alaska. My father would be reading the map and we would be in the Yukon somewhere, lost. When we stopped for the night, my mother would set up an easel and do a painting of a moose or a mountain. My father would cook supper over an open fire. I liked to think that all of this was happening right now in some sort of alternate timeline or parallel universe. My family is lost on a small back road in the Yukon. I can smell the shish kebab my father is cooking. There are mosquitoes the size of model airplanes but they are not biting. My sister is doing her nails. I am thinking about fishing. My father and I talk about going fishing, but we never really do it because we don't like having to kill fish.

"Holy shit!" my parallel father suddenly screeches out loud. One of the model airplane mosquitoes has bitten him on the neck. The shish kebab stick he had been wielding goes flying into the wilderness and probably lands on a moose turd the size of a squashed basketball.

After school I had to go for my visit with Dave. He had this once a week thing going. I never fully decided if I liked the idea of counselling. But I liked Dave and he was unconventional. All the kids at school knew I was going to the weirdest shrink around and some of them started asking their parents if they could go for counselling too, but most got turned down because Dave was fairly expensive. Three trips to Dave or a new TV set for your room? a parent might ask. Parents didn't want other people to know that their kid was going to a shrink, anyway, especially one who was recommending things like smoking as a cure for what ails you.

Dave always believed in the tangential approach. "I like to vector in, aim for the perimeter of the problem, not the bull's eye," he'd say.

"Today we do that word association thing," he said when I got there.

"I'm in."

"Dice?" he said.

"Gambling."

"White?"

"Snow."

"Horses?"

"Jupiter."

"Christmas?"

"Avalanche."

"Water?"

"Desert."

"Ink?"

"Paper."

"Window?"

"Opportunity."

"Table?"

"Knife."

"Family?"

"Robots."

"Car?"

I almost said "keys," but something stopped me and I didn't know what. Without thinking I put my hand in my pocket, still thinking about car keys. Car keys in my pocket. But it didn't make any sense.

Dave saw the puzzled look on my face. "Well, enough of that anyway. You had a few interesting creative responses. Non-traditional, in some cases. I like that. Why don't you tell me a bit about how things are going."

"Things are going well. The universe is unfolding as it should."

"What did you do yesterday?"

"School?"

"What happened at school?"

"Nothing."

"There's a fresh response."

"Well, you know."

"What about last night? What did you do?"

"Same old thing."

"Which is?"

That's when I realized that I couldn't exactly recall what I did last night. It was a nothing night. "I guess I did some homework, listened to the radio. I must have gone to bed early."

Dave was looking at me in that Dave sort of way. Then he tugged at his ponytail and looked out the window. "Know anything about Salvador Dali?"

"Yeah, he was way out there. Melting watches over the branches of trees. Some kind of painter. Spanish, right? Big moustache."

"I wanted to look up something about Dali, so I check out a couple of search engines. One keeps taking me to this really interesting site where I find all these paintings. Dali, Picasso, some other stuff that's unlabelled. I click on something called 'Stuff to Consider,' and I get this little lesson about something called 'neutron soup.' Are you familiar with neutron soup?"

"Sure. Collapsed stars, electrons rammed into protons. So dense that a piece the size of a sugar cube would weigh a thousand million tons."

"Right." Pony-tug. "Then I check the web address and discover it's something called Emerso.com."

"Probably an acronym."

Dave looked out the window. "So I'm there staring at my computer monitor — you know I'm not that savvy about all this Internet stuff. A rank amateur compared to you kids. But I'm thinking this weird site is strangely familiar. It's like a public version of a public version of the images and the ideas of a single very singular person."

"Darrell was too good."

"The Egg Man?"

"He built the site with so many tags placed so perfectly that most of the search engines will send you to me in the first five listings. You typed in 'Dali' and wham, you were at Emerso and began to root around. You could have typed in 'soup' hoping for a recipe for turkey noodle and end up reading about black holes and collapsed stars."

"You scanned the paintings?" Dave asked.

"Sure. Dali, Picasso. Lots of Hieronymus Bosch."

"Figures," Dave said. "I made a little tour of your gallery. Very impressive. How come some were unidentified?"

"Just sloppy web mastering, I guess."

"But it's a great site. How many people know you created it?"

"It's a secret between Darrell and me. He set it up but I put in the content."

"Very eclectic. But why the secrecy?"

"I don't know. I like the idea of communicating with people over the net. I get to put my ideas and some borrowed stuff out there but nobody knows who I am."

"They get a sense of who you are by what you're interested in."

"Then maybe that's who I really am. I'm Emerso. Martin is the kid who sits in the third seat in the second row in English class. I can be both, can't I?"

"Yes. You are both. You are one hell of a kid. I enjoy talking with you. You challenge me. You challenge people on your website, too. Time's about up. Anything bothering you this week? Anything make you mad?"

"Not really."

"Damn."

At home, I logged onto Yahoo. I typed in "Hieronymus Bosch" and it listed nearly 750 sites. Mine was number six. I clicked on it and saw the familiar *Garden of Earthly Delights,* where people are part human, part animal, part vegetable. This bizarre and far-fetched image seemed to be a kind of explanation for many of the kids and teachers at school.

I clicked on "Art" and it gave me screen after screen of dozens of miniature paintings. I remember all the hours I'd put in scanning them from books. I don't know why it seemed so important that my site had these paintings. They all could be found elsewhere on the Internet. But what gave me a funny feeling on the fifth page of the catalogue was the painting made by my mother, the one she had called *Alaskan Sunrise*, but there was no title or name listed here. I clicked on the next page and found more of her paintings. No artist name again, no title.

No one else but me could have scanned the paintings from the photos and posted them here. But I couldn't remember doing it.

I went back to *Alaskan Sunrise* and maximized the image. There was a mountain and a forest and something half-realized in the foreground that could have been a van with a family standing around a campfire. Or it could have been something else.

CHAPTER NINE

Nobody ever said good things about school, but I found school to be a safe, goofy place. I had perhaps inherited the ability to be invisible from my father, and after my brief career of notoriety — smoking, egg tossing, and eco-warrior random kindness activist — I returned to being comfortable as a kind of nobody. I just wasn't cut out to be a troublemaker and I was too smart to be cleverly stupid like some kids who became famous for doing really dumb things at school.

I had a basic sense of doing the right thing that made me appear dull to others. I handed in homework; I did well on tests. I had a genuine interest in things like the periodic table and cell mitosis. I liked reading long books by dead English writers. Darrell had similar faults — he was extremely good at math and was a natural at learning foreign languages. He always got an A in French but he studied Russian and Greek on the side. No one knew why, not even Darrell. He disliked Latin because he found it too easy. "No wonder their civilization crumbled," he said once, referring to the fact their language was overly structured and ultimately uninteresting.

Most kids, if they thought about me at all, still had some sympathy for me over the death of my mother. I think everyone wondered what it would be like to lose his or her own mother. But if anyone asked me about it, I used a stock response: "It was really bad for a while, but I'm over the worst of it." Those were words that just came out. I couldn't explain what it was that I was feeling over her death. I had created firewalls around that part of my life. Necessary barriers that allowed me to get on with things. Dave knew all about my defences, he said, and he thought that I needed to take a big sledgehammer to those walls. But I wasn't ready. Maybe I never would be.

Mr. Cohen, the vice principal, had a special interest in me. He was a nice guy, which was a poor qualification for a VP who had to deal with trouble. He would stop me in the hall and ask me how I was doing. "Martin, how is it going?"

"Not bad."

"What is it you are reading these days?" Mr. Cohen loved books and he knew I read voraciously.

"Jules Verne. *Journey to the Centre of the Earth*."

"Have your read *The Island of Dr. Moreau* yet?"

"It's next on my list."

"I want you to let me know what you think about the ethical issues involved — about vivisection, as they used to call it, and ramifications to cloning and genetic mapping."

"I will do that. See you later, Mr. Cohen."

"Take care."

See what I mean? School was a goofy, warm place. Where else would I have such a conversation?

I had an interest in a girl. It was a long-term thing, a kind of unrequited affair of the heart with Kathy Bringhurst. Kathy was not beautiful in the twentieth-century high school girl sort of way. I think they would have thought she was pretty in the nineteenth century, though. She had a nineteenth-century nose and cheek-bones and a very pale complexion. An eggshell complexion, as Darrell pointed out. She was smart but pretended not to be and she was always interested in some really good-looking guy who wouldn't give her the time of day. A guy like Scott Rutledge.

Back before Mom died, I had a true crush on Kathy and had tried (and failed miserably) several times to explain to her how I felt. I even resorted to writing a poem for her — words spilled straight from the heart in rhyming couplets like they might have done in the nineteenth century. I sealed it in an envelope with a wax seal from a candle and gave it to her during Heavy Metal Math class.

"Don't open it until you get home."

She had looked at me in a warm, fuzzy way and stuffed the envelope in her math book. The next day she said she had lost the envelope walking home. "It must have fallen out of my book bag." She blinked and asked me what had been in it.

"Nothing important," I said.

Nowadays she was interested in Scott Rutledge. All the girls were interested in Scott. Scott broke hearts left, right, and centre. It was who he was. Kathy was not up to Scott's standards and she knew it, but instead of turning her gaze elsewhere, she pined for Scott in an old-fashioned sort of way. I was her biggest confidant. She told me if Scott had talked to her or shown any small courtesy. I would pretend interest. She was almost in tears once because she thought Scott was about to ask her out before he lost interest and moved on to Katie Osmond.

My passion, if that's the right word, for Kathy had diminished to a small hopeful flame. Hopeful maybe is not the right word. After the loss of the wax-sealed envelope, I saw things as hopeless except for the fact that Kathy considered me a "friend," and so I would suffer Scott stories for eternity or until I graduated, whichever came first. Dave had once asked me if Kathy reminded me in any way of my mother. And I had said, "Definitely not."

"Do they share any physical resemblance?"

I had never thought about it. I could picture Kathy with her fragile, pale face and sad eyes. But I couldn't even remember what my mother looked like and that scared the hell out of me. "Not at all," I told Dave. "What's with this Sigmund Freud thing?"

"Sorry, dude," he said. "Guess I got carried away."

Like I said, I sat beside Kathy Bringhurst during Heavy Metal Math class. Mr. Miller, the former lead guitar of the now defunct band Gangrene, had his guitar in class today. Everyone was very attentive. Mr. Miller had enlarged his notion of math teaching to include "logic" in the curriculum. Some parents, for some unknown reason, had complained about this, and Mr. Miller had to defend himself at a parent-teacher meeting. Mr. Miller, as mentioned, was also a former wrestling champion in that world of show-off half-fake, half-real Saturday afternoon wrestling. (Someone had found magazine pictures of him mud wrestling and some kids had forged his nickname: Heavy Metal Mud Wrestling Math Teacher).

After the parents had met Mr. Miller, the fathers had convinced the mothers that it was probably okay for him to enlarge the math curriculum to include logic, or even astrology, voodoo, or atheism if he was so inclined.

So Mr. Miller had his old Fender guitar plugged into his "practice" amp. He hit a ragged, soft humming distorted minor chord and played a riff on the high E string that I knew came from one of Gangrene's early hits and then he said, "I first learned about something called the 'gambler's fallacy' when we were touring with Aerosmith. We were the opening act. Aerosmith was very unprofessional in my opinion back then. Drunk and rude and never on time and sometimes their instruments weren't even in tune. They had no true respect for the audience.

"Well, to get to the point, before a big gig in, um, Minneapolis one night, you-know-who asked me if I had a quarter. I dug in my pocket and found him one. He began to flip the coin. You'd think a superstar like that would have better things to do with his time than flip a coin for ten to twenty minutes at a time, but he didn't.

"'Bucky boy, I want you to watch this,' he said. He called me Bucky boy back then. I don't know why. He refused to use my real name.

"'I've flipped this coin seven times,' he said, 'and it's always come up heads. You were paying attention right?' Well, not really. 'Let's see what happens. Stay with me.'"

HMMWMT hit a couple of power chords, ran his fingers up and down the neck of the guitar to move from several high staccato squeals to a low-pitched thunder — all of which must have been driving the other teachers in the hall mad.

"So he continues to flip the coin, promising me it's a real coin — a 'fair' coin as he called it. He flipped it five more times and it came up heads each time. Then he said he wanted to make me a bet. Seven hundred dollars. He bet seven hundred dollars that the coin would turn up heads again.

"'It's some kind of trick you do, right?' I asked.

"'You flip the bleedin' quarter then,' he said. 'Are you in on the bet?'

"He had flipped what appeared to be a regular quarter twelve times and it had come up heads each time. I figured the odds were well in my favour that the next flip would be tails. So I went for the bet. I flipped the quarter and let it land on the floor."

Mr. Miller tromped on his effects pedal and closed his eyes as he played a short but effective guitar blitzkrieg.

"I lost seven hundred dollars that day but learned a very important lesson of logic. The gambler's fallacy. I fell for it. I thought the odds were, um, maybe ninety percent that the next flip would be tails but, in reality, the odds were still fifty percent. He could have won or I could have won. And if he had lost seven hundred clams, what would it be to him? But I lost. I haven't gambled since."

The bell rang then before he could hit a final chord. The HMMWMT turned off the power to his amp. "Tomorrow I'll tell you about the liar's paradox, and if we have time, we'll nail down some of the ideas put forward by Immanuel Kant."

So this is why school was not such a horrible place to spend the day.

CHAPTER TEN

♄ ♄ ♄

Meaning of Life

You probably haven't spent a lot of time thinking about Immanuel Kant. This is because he was a German philoso-pher who lived in the eighteenth century. Philosophers spend a lot of time thinking instead of watching television, but this is obvious in Immanuel's case because they had no TV back then. He wrote a lot about ethics, which is the science of telling right from wrong.

We make ethical (or unethical) decisions every day, even every minute of our lives, and each of us has our own set of ethics that we follow.

Immanuel Kant was really into this ethical thing and trying to figure out the meaning of life. I don't want this to turn into a big rant on Kant except to say that he saw every individual as an end, not a means. In contemporary terms, this suggests that we are all here for a purpose. We are here for a reason.

That makes a person feel pretty good about him- or herself, but the problem is that we probably never figure out what that reason is. Some people pretend to be confident about who they are and what they are all about, but I think that's mostly a front.

I think most of us are confused. We are baffled. We are searching. And it doesn't matter if we find answers or not. The searching and questioning is the important thing.

⚡ ⚡ ⚡

Dave had been after me to get my father to open up. My father was working way too much and when he came home he appeared exhausted. He planted himself in front of the tube and watched basketball or football, or hockey or tennis or golf.

He was a good father, I know, but since Mom died he had shut his life down. Lilly and I didn't know what to do about it. She shopped and stocked the refrigerator and pantry with lots of food and we fended for ourselves. If my father ate at all, he didn't do it on the premises. Coffee and maybe three bites out of a bagel in the morning. At night, he came home claiming to have consumed something — although he never said what — at the office.

Then he did the TV plant. When the power went out one night, he just sat on the sofa watching the empty screen.

One time I was taking out the trash and I accidentally dumped the big green plastic can in the driveway. Out spilled a whole bunch of photographs, some of them torn — of him, of her, of us. I took the trash can back into the garage and went through the whole mess. I saved old movie stubs of the original *Star Wars*, which he must have gone to with Mom. There was a lock of her hair. There were old letters they had sent to each other before they were married. And a lot more.

I salvaged what I could and took it back to my room. I taped up the photos. It was like putting our lives back together. I cleaned everything up and put it into a box. Some day he would want this back.

I lay on my bed staring at a picture of me as a toddler. I could only find half of the picture. There was me on my feet with two outstretched adult arms holding me up, keeping me from falling. I looked very unstable. The look on my face suggested I wasn't used to having my head so far above my feet. But, aside from the arms, the rest of my mother was missing from the picture. She'd been ripped away.

I was thinking about shutting down my website because I thought I was getting a little too weird, writing about a German philosopher, getting all cerebral, but it was getting a lot of hits these days. Darrell had added some great 3-D graphics. Maybe that was all that kept people coming back to it.

CHAPTER ELEVEN

"Gottfried Wilhelm Leibniz. Does that name ring a bell for any of you?" Mr. Miller asked.

"Did he play drums for Rush?" Scott Rutledge asked.

"That was Mr. Neil Peart. You're way off."

"Bass player for AC/DC?"

"Not even getting warm."

But the class was warmer. HMMWMT always had a way of loosening up an otherwise uptight and irascible group of young people. I wasn't about to raise my hand. I knew who Leibniz was but I knew better than to open my yap and draw attention. I had inherited some of my father's skills of being invisible and I used them when I wanted to.

"Our friend Gottfried Leibniz came up with something we call differential calculus. Actually differential and integral calculus. He and good old Isaac, Mr. I-discovered-gravity Newton. But Leibniz was really into math."

"Surprise, surprise," Scott Rutledge added.

"Well, the surprise is that he also came up with the concept that we — us, you and me, all of us — live in the best of all possible worlds."

"Right." It was Scott again.

"Did I detect a bit of sarcasm in that reply, Mr. Rutledge?"

"Just a tad."

The class loved this sort of dialogue and so did Mr. Miller. "Don't worry, I'll get on to the important stuff in a minute — going over your homework, that is. Everybody who did your homework raise your hand."

Most hands went up. HMMWMT, as was his habit, counted. "I counted thirty-one out of thirty-five, if you were all honest. And I know you are honest because you all promised, one hundred percent of you, back in September that you would live by my code of ethics: be honest, be cool, be yourself. Thirty-one out of thirty-five. That's 88.572 percent if I round it off to the third decimal place."

I saw Darrell slide his calculator out from under his desk and check the math. He looked at me and gave me a thumb's up. We didn't know how Mr. Miller did it, but the guy was way out there when it came to math. Math and philosophy.

"Back to Leibniz. Another one of the old German intellectual types. Lived in the last half of the seventeenth century. The good old days. No distractions. People lived their whole lives, some of them, just using their brains to think up stuff. Like Leibniz here. He said we live in the best of all possible worlds. Why? First, because he believed in God. How many of you believe in God?"

Another count. "Twenty-five."

Darrell checked his watch. The class held its communal breath.

"That would be 71.4285 percent."

I looked over at Darrell. He silently mouthed the words, "Three seconds." Mr. Miller was a human computer.

Scott raised his hand again. "Mr. Miller, I'm not sure you should count me in. I'm not sure I believe in God."

"We call that agnostic."

"Whatever."

"I'll leave it for now because I need to get back to Leibniz. He did believe in God, he had no doubts whatsoever, and he was certain God was not only good but all-knowing and all-powerful. Therefore, if you follow my drift, God could only create a perfect world. Leibniz, if he were here right now to say it himself, would assure you that you live in that perfect world. Every darn thing that happens is right and good."

"That's a bit hard to swallow," said Scott, speaking on behalf of the class. All the girls looked at him when he had anything to say.

"Because you, Mr. Rutledge, are not Gottfried Leibniz. You're an agnostic. You have doubts."

"So you are saying, if I woke up Monday morning and my head was all fuzzy from too much partying and it was cold and rainy and ugly outside and I had to get up out of my warm bed and go to school, then that would be perfect."

"Precisely, because it is a perfect world. Things appear to you and me, because we are mortal, less than perfect. But that's only because our minds are limited in scope."

I cribbed some juicy stuff from the HMMWMT for my website but I was afraid I might start losing my audience if I waxed on about too many German philosophers. So I promised myself to poke around for some other divergent ideas and interests.

Unfortunately, that very evening I was stuck in the living room with Jake while he was waiting for my sister to get ready to go out. Jake sat on the sofa looking at really stupid music videos. He was a big fan of any video that involved spitting, swearing, or guys sniffing their armpits.

I admit, I liked to taunt Jake with anything remotely intellectual. I hit the mute button and launched into Leibniz.

"Where do you get this wacko stuff from? You been watching the Learning Channel or something?"

"No. School."

"I never heard of anyone talking about stuff like this in school."

"Maybe you haven't been paying attention."

"School is like prison. You go in, they lock the doors, and you put in time. They unlock the doors, you go out. That's what school is."

"Leibniz would say it's all part of the perfect world."

"You need help."

"I'm already seeing a shrink."

"Oh, yeah, how's Dave?"

"Dave is good."

"He have any more advice for you? Suggest any new hobbies like shoplifting or purse snatching?" Jake grabbed the remote and clicked on the sound of a video that employed a heck of a lot of snakes.

Lilly arrived downstairs. She had her black lipstick on, which I thought made her look ghoulish. It was complemented by a heavy red eye shadow and some kind of makeup that made the rest of her face look ultra pale.

"Sweet," Jake said.

"Don't wait up for me," she told me. And they were out the door.

Some of us caught it on the TV news Sunday night. Others didn't know until first thing Monday morning. It wasn't raining but it was cold and the sky was heavy and low with bruised-looking clouds. Before long, everyone in the school had heard the news: Scott Rutledge had proven his mortality by getting killed in an accident.

He'd been riding on the back of his brother's motorcycle, no helmet. His brother was showing off. There was a curve in the road, a dog. You could read all about it in the newspaper. It was all part of the perfection of the world.

If it had been anyone else, the school would have mourned, but it was more than that with Scott. Scott had been the golden boy. The girls had crushes, sure, but he had no enemies. He had looks, intelligence, and a way with everyone. If he'd made it to graduation, he would have been slotted for best-looking, friend to all, and that absurdly coveted most likely to succeed.

The principal called for an "extended homeroom" to allow kids to adjust to the news. Homeroom teachers cleared their throats and tried to say significant things about the death of Scott. Some stumbled over words, a few mouthed platitudes. One of them led her students in prayer.

Finally a bell rang, and we were to go to our second-period class, having skipped the first of the day. Kathy grabbed me in the hall by her locker. She had been crying. "Walk with me. I'm not going to class. Let's sit in the cafeteria."

"Sure."

We sat, the two of us, in the empty cafeteria. I wanted to tell her how much I cared for her. I wanted to tell her how screwed up the world was, how wrong everything was. I wanted to tell her that there was no meaning to anything.

"I think Scott was going to ask me out," she said.

"You two had been spending time together?"

She shook her head. "No. It's not that. It's just this feeling I had. Scott had been interested in all those other girls but it never lasted."

"He played the field."

"But it would have been different with me. He knew that."

"Yeah."

"And now he's gone. I'll never see him again."

I wanted to tell her that I knew for a fact that the odds are against graduating high school without at least one or two of your classmates dying from something. Funny that it had to be Scott. Had it been Darrell or me everyone would have felt bad, then been mystified that they had never really known or understood us. People would have felt bad that they had not taken the time to get to know us while were alive and now we were gone. It would have been a tragedy, but we would have faded from memory quickly, I think, almost as if we had never been there.

But not Scott.

"Kathy, I think Scott was a fool for not asking you out earlier." I was fishing for a way to say something about my own feelings for her.

"Scott was Scott. He liked all the attention. I was just part of the crowd."

"You were never just part of the crowd."

"I think I was in love with him," Kathy said.

I knew that Scott would loom large in her life, whatever she did from here on. A dog on a street and a motorcycle out of control and a martyr for love bleeding out his lifeblood on a stretch of suburban pavement. And Kathy, maybe forever, locked into what might have been — even if it was mostly in her imagination. I touched her hand and she looked up at me. Her eyes were wet with tears.

"Martin, what do I do now?"

"Want me to call your parents and get them to come pick you up?"

"No."

"Martin?"

"What?"

"Hold me."

The door opened to the cafeteria and Mr. Egan, our guidance counsellor, stepped through. He saw Martin

Emerson with his arms around Kathy Bringhurst. She had her head on Martin's shoulder and she was sobbing. Mr. Egan gingerly closed the cafeteria door again and walked away.

I remember the feeling of Kathy's tears soaking through my cotton shirt and I could feel the warm wet spot on my shoulder. She had her arms around me and did not let go for the longest while. My heart was beating very fast and I didn't want this to end. I did not cry or feel the need to cry. I think I had felt terrible about Scott's death. Unlike Gottfried Leibniz, I had been thinking the world was this big stupid, pointless place where ridiculous, cruel things happened to anyone at random.

Now, it was different. Sitting there in the empty cafeteria holding onto Kathy, I was feeling pretty good. Despite what had brought us to this, I was holding Kathy Bringhurst in my arms. And I felt more alive than I'd felt in a long time. And for that, a surge of guilt swept over me like a tidal wave. But I did not let go of her until another bell rang and it was time to leave before the swarm of kids came through the door for study hall.

We walked together to math class and sat in our usual seats. Kathy was in the back alongside the empty desk that people kept looking at. Mr. Miller closed the door. His guitar case was on the teacher's desk, his amp in front of the blackboard. He plugged in the guitar and turned the amp on, then hit a loud, angry distorted chord. His amp was way loud, insanely piercing. He hit the chord again and again and then began to play some kind of crazy riff — high and squealy and soulful. It was angry and sad and so full of hurt that it swept us all away.

It reminded me of an old Jimi Hendrix song that Darrell had downloaded for me from the Internet. Mr. Miller's guitar blasting away there in school shattered the silence that had loomed all morning. He wasn't looking at us as he played; he looked down at the floor. It was the most mournful, piercing sound imaginable and he kept playing, even after the door opened and Mr. Cohen and two other teachers stood there looking at him.

He played faster and harder, and the whole scene was way too weird for us to comprehend, but it was becoming clear that Mr. Miller had been deeply affected by the death of his student and was having some kind of breakdown.

He hit one final dissonant chord and then took off his guitar, raised it above his head, and then smashed it down hard on his desk. The neck broke off the body of the guitar and the amp let go with a long wail of feedback as he threw what was left of his guitar down on the floor and walked out the door, past Mr. Cohen and the other teachers.

By noon that day, the principal had called off school and sent everybody home early. On the bus ride home, my own thoughts were confused. I felt really bad about

Scott. But I also felt a little envious of the attention he was getting even though he was dead. I realized that I was feeling jealous and I was annoyed at myself for feeling that way.

CHAPTER TWELVE

The Universe

Most people don't spend a lot of time worrying about the difference between the cosmos and the universe. Some would say they are the same thing, just two different words. One accepted definition of the universe is that it is the sum total of all material things. Well, you can see the limitations with that. The universe is just the stuff that is physical and if you are the kind of person who has been spending your time hanging around this website, you already know that matter is 99.99 percent nothing. Little chunks of supposed matter — protons, neutrons, pi mesons, and all their cousins spinning around so fast that we think they are something but they're probably just a bunch of energy. Well, you get my drift.

For the sake of argument, though, we can assume that the universe is like the hammer. You can pick it up and it has weight and seems to exist in the material sense. If you had a giant hand, you could pick it up and whack something with it and it would have an impact. If the universe hit the thumb of some imaginary giant (and I do mean a truly gargantuan) hand, then it would hurt like hell because of the supposed matter packed together in the hammer head.

Now, for the sake of argument again, I'd say the cosmos is something more ambiguous and grander. It includes everything that exists (or appears to exist in the physical sense) but all the other junk too. All ideas, all desires, all memories of swimming in a pond when you were a kid, all thoughts as well as hammers. A thought is a kind of hammer, actually, which is a metaphor you might want to pursue on your own time.

So the universe is a small sort of ghetto for debatable material things and the cosmos is the big anything-goes warehouse. You couldn't easily pick up the cosmos and use it like a hammer. It's more like a big fish net for catching things.

One dictionary suggests that cosmos implies an "orderly system." Which this critic finds annoying. Whose order? Why does it have to be orderly? Probably because language is in the business of making things orderly, which makes us feel very clever. We put things in boxes with language — it's like organizing your old baseball cards according to team or batting average. Fun to do for a while but tedious and somewhat pointless after a bit.

The only good thing about the dictionary is that it has a second meaning for cosmos: "A tall garden plant with varying coloured flowers resembling a daisy." I didn't get it at first. I thought it was some kind of linguistic joke. A cosmic joke. But if I can suggest the universe is a hammer, then why can't the cosmos be a flower?

That's a rhetorical question, by the way. Please don't try to send me e-mails with your answers. Talk it up in the Emerso chat room if you like. Anything goes in the chat room, as long as there is a degree of common courtesy and mutual respect. Even if the universe is made up of 99.99 percent emptiness, I still believe that people should be nice to each other.

Emerso

My mother grew flowers in a large flower bed out the back door. Some flowers came back year after year. Some she started from seed. She knew the names of all of them. When I was little, I sat on the back steps with a couple of toy trucks and pretended I was a truck driver. Why I thought truck driving was such a great job, I don't know. But my life's goal was to grow up and drive a truck all over North America. What could be more exciting, I thought, than driving a real truck? So I sat on the back steps and drove a tractor-trailer to someplace. I knew lots of names of places because I was a weird little kid who memorized things from any book I could find. I had learned to read at a shockingly premature age.

I also studied the maps in a big atlas at night.

"Where are you driving to today?" my mother would ask while she was planting some kind of bulb.

"Norway," I would answer, or "Zimbabwe." My trucks could go over oceans and up the sides of mountains. I lived in the realm of possibility, not actuality. I wouldn't have to cope with tangible reality checks and roadblocks until I was older.

"What is your cargo?"

"Light bulbs," I would answer, or sometimes, "Plutonium." Plutonium was one of my favourite words.

"Where are you going to drive to tomorrow?"

"Bangladesh and then Ohio."

And so it went.

Sometimes I just moved my lips like kids do, trying to make the sound of a diesel engine by blowing air out through pursed lips. During such moments, my mother would talk to her plants instead of me. She believed talking to plants made them grow better.

"How are the nasturtiums today?" I remember her saying. "And you, the delphiniums?"

She looked at them as if truly expecting an answer.

Sometimes I would stop motor mouthing and she would point a finger at each flower and name it: "Peony, tulip, calendula, marigold, gladioli, lily, delphinium, daisy, iris, poppy, cosmos."

Mr. Miller was not in school the next day and the sub-stitute teacher, Ms. Schencks, said he was taking some time off. By the end of school day, the truth was out: the HMMWMT had been told he had to take a leave — he was suspended. Some parents had complained that he had gone over the top. Some teachers had suggest-ed that he had gone off the deep end. Kathy suggested to me that something about the death of Scott had pushed him over the edge.

In study hall, I sat beside Kathy and waited for her to start up one of our whispered conversations. I was expecting to hear a lot more about how she felt about losing Scott, the Scott she had never really had.

"I'm mad at him, you know. He should have told me how he felt before... before this."

I understood this thing about being mad, because that was what Dave was always talking about. My problem. I never got mad about anything. Even, well, you know.

"I know he didn't think I was as attractive as Kelly Tyler or Jen Greenlaw but I think he was beginning to appreciate my other qualities."

"You are probably the smartest girl in the class."

"I'm not that smart. Besides, I don't really want to be smart. I want to be thought of as mysterious."

Kathy was as mysterious to me as all the other girls I knew. I wanted to say something complimentary so I took the hook. "I bet you're more mysterious than all the other girls in this study hall."

"You think I'm more mysterious even than Sybil over there?"

Sybil was a tough one to pick. She was mysterious. She wore dark clothes like Lilly and cultivated a pale and humourless demeanour. She listened only to music that she called "experimental" and she kept a lot to herself, reading books on shamanism.

"Anybody can be like Sybil. She's not mysterious at all. Compared to you."

"Why do you think I'm mysterious?"

Uh oh. I was not a great conversationalist or a very good bullshitter. I tried to imagine how Scott might have handled this. Scott was born with charm and tact and verbal skills stitched right onto his chromosomes. I was born only with a high IQ and quirky interests. I tried to smile like Scott would have smiled. "You have a look about you."

"I do?"

"Yeah. Something unfathomable."

"Wow."

Mr. Willis was tapping his pointer stick on the table in front of us. Time to shut up. Mr. Willis never spoke at all during study hall. He only tapped with a pointer stick or a ruler or sometimes smacked a book down loud so that it made a great walloomph sound in the high-ceilinged cafeteria where we had afternoon study hall. He saved me from having to rifle through the thesaurus in my brain for more big words. I didn't know why Kathy wanted to be mysterious. She wasn't any more mysterious than the rest, but I still had my feelings for her, so I would go home and work on a list of compliments to throw her way: cryptic, enigmatic, perplexing, and paradoxical, but unfathomable was a good start.

Mr. Egan had called Dave to tell him that they believed I might be "at risk" over the death of Scott. I give credit to all the teachers and neighbours who worried about my mental well-being. I suppose, in my own way, I was paradoxical, enigmatic, cryptic, and, to some, unfathomable. If they knew about my website and some of the stuff I rambled on about, they would probably try to put me in a loony bin.

Dave seemed kind of nervous when I went for my next visit. He was eating a tofu and tuna fish sandwich and apologized. "I had to schedule you on my lunch break. Want half?"

"S'okay. You didn't really need to see me."

"Well, I'm your shrink. Bob Egan had some concerns. Wanna tell me about it?"

I told him about Scott. About how it made me feel. I told him about the HMMWMT getting suspended. "What is it Mr. Egan thinks I will do?"

"He thinks that sometimes things like this push a kid over the edge."

"Or an adult."

"Adults too."

"They shouldn't have suspended Mr. Miller. Now they say he's not coming back at all. Parents don't trust him. Playing electric guitar in class wasn't normal, they said."

"It's not fair, is it?"

"He was the best teacher in the school."

"What about you? How do you feel about Scott?"

"I feel guilty because I was jealous of him. And when I heard he was gone, I realized that Kathy might pay more attention to me rather than him. I'm sorry I feel that way."

"That's okay. Guilt is good. In its own way. It doesn't have to last. It's one way to deal with the loss. Let it evolve into something positive."

A typical Dave way of saying something.

"I suppose."

"Are you going to go to his funeral?"

"No."

"Any idea why?"

"We weren't really that close or anything."

"I was just asking."

Dave nibbled his sandwich. "We haven't talked about your mother for a while."

"I could see this coming a mile off."

"You don't want to talk bout it?"

"No, it's okay."

"You been to her grave?"

"Not since she was buried." But as soon as the words were out, they felt like a lie. I guess it showed on my face.

"What is it?"

"I don't know. Maybe you made me feel guilty about not going there."

"Why do you think people go to graveyards after they lose someone?"

"Personal reasons, I guess." I was working on fire-walls and not sure why.

"Very personal, I'm sure. But I want you to go there, okay? It's been a while."

"She's not there. That's just her body. I don't see the point."

"Maybe there is no point. It's up to you."

Dave finished his sandwich. "You think I can tell Mr. Egan you are okay? Safe. No big complications — about Scott I mean."

"Yeah, I'm okay with that. I'll be all right. I'll get over my guilt thing and all that."

"Cool."

On the bus ride home, I tried to picture the gravesite in the cemetery but I couldn't see it. It was as if I had never been there, not even at the funeral. But I could picture in my head the route from my house to the cemetery clear as day. I could see every street, every stop sign, the houses and stores along the way. I had a kind of sick feeling in my stomach.

When I got home I sat down on the back steps and looked at the flower bed. It was grown over with weeds and the flowers were unhealthy looking, some of them dead. "I'm sorry," I said to them, sorry for letting them go unattended. I leaned over and began to yank out big clumps of weeds. And I tried to remember the names of the flowers: delphinium, marigold, peony, lily, gladioli, cosmos.

I remembered with crystal clarity the conversation of a small boy sitting on those back steps with his mother.

"Where are you driving to today?"

"Norway."

CHAPTER THIRTEEN

Junk

There are four and a half million people in Norway and I don't know even one of them. I wonder what it's like in Norway in the winter when it stays dark for almost all of the day. It's like that in the Northwest Territories, too, they say. I think I'd freak over that.

Why you should be interested in Norway, I don't know. They were Vikings at one time and they had lots of wars. In a war, people kill other people on purpose. They think they are doing the right thing by killing their enemy. You would expect that we would have evolved past that by now but we haven't. I don't think the Norwegians do a lot of organized killing anymore, but some countries still do. The list is too long to include here.

There are thousands of islands that are part of Norway. On many of those islands you could live a very isolated, peaceful life. But it might get lonely sometimes in the depths of a dark, cold winter.

Emerso

I was sitting in the cafeteria at lunch hour with Darrell. "Sorry I didn't call you back last night after you left that message," I said. "I get confused sometimes."

"Confusion is good. The state prior to enlightenment, said one Chinese philosopher."

"Scott Rutledge never looked confused. He always looked like he knew what he was doing. Like he understood what was going on."

"I could never be like that."

"Me neither," I agreed.

"Many hits on your site?"

I nodded. "Lots of people out there killing time."

"Killing time. Ever think about why we say it that way?"

"It's weird isn't it?"

"Lotta stuff is weird. I'm thinking that maybe it's too weird and we'll never figure it out. Not enough time."

"Tempus fugit."

"Exactly." Darrell paused, looked toward the fluo-rescent lights like he was waiting for a message from some alien friends. Then he shook his head. "I just don't know what the methodology is. It's really tragic about Scott. Martin, if you could make a trade, I mean if we could manipulate time and space and stuff, and you could trade your life as you are now, alive and breathing, for having lived the life of Scott Rutledge — you know with his looks, the girls, and all that — but now you're dead — would you do it?"

Leave it to Darrell to pose such a question. I didn't have to think twice. "Yes."

"Me too."

"Too much killing time, I guess. Darrell, if I tell you something, would you promise not to tell anyone?"

"My lips are sealed."

"I think I know how to drive."

Junk

The imagination has teeth. You bite into a thing and chew on it. You leave marks in what you are chewing. You process reality this way. You chew it, you taste it with your tongue, and then you swallow it and it becomes part of you or it ends up as shit.

The line between what is real and what is imagined is a fuzzy line. It's all based on perception. Just because we can't see it with our eyes doesn't mean it doesn't exist. You don't see the electromagnetic waves coming at your television set, do you? But they are real. (This is if you have the old antenna thing and not just cable.)

In the end, what is real and what is not real is probably less important than what you believe. I believe life would be much better for me in Norway, for example, but I have never been there. I don't speak Norwegian and I don't have Viking blood. I may not feel at all at home around Norwegians but I wouldn't mind living on one of those thousand islands off the coast. When it got dark in the winter for days at a time, I would sit inside with my imagination and be content.

If you want something to do, sit in a totally dark room and write down what goes through your head. Don't use paper with lines on it because you won't be able to see the lines. Your writing will be sloppy and go all over the place, but I think you'll be able to make sense of it later.

Leonardo Da Vinci wrote notes in his notebook backwards by looking at his handwriting in a mirror. Some think this was for secrecy, but that sounds lame. Probably, it was more a matter of trying to make his brain work in different ways. Leonardo Da Vinci, they say, was curious about everything. He was curious about water bugs and stars, but he also invented new styles of clothing and horribly effective instruments of war. He designed a really evil-looking military tank with sharp spikes sticking out on all sides to pierce anybody who came close. Inside the tank were horses that moved it along. It was a long time ago.

Curiosity invented the nuclear bomb. It's hard to come to a conclusion about whether curiosity is a good thing or bad thing for a human being. It probably all depends on what kind of human being you are.

Emerso

Lilly announced she was breaking up with Jake. This was an oft-repeated performance.

"Congratulations. He's a weasel."

"Shut up. You don't know anything."

"Lilly, be nice to your brother. He's under a lot of stress." It was my father, passing through the kitchen on his way to the TV set in the living room.

"Dad, I think we should move to Alaska," Lilly shouted, but he was already out of the room.

"Maybe next week," he said from a distance.

"I guess Jake was okay," I conceded. A bold-faced lie.

"Jake is irresponsible, inconsiderate, rude, self-centred, stupid, irritating, cruel, and he doesn't like to take showers."

"Yeah, but I mean aside from that, he was okay."

Lilly smiled. I had forgotten what she looked like when she smiled. It was Mom's smile, but I didn't say that out loud.

"Want a coffee?" she asked.

"French vanilla cappuccino, maybe."

So we walked down to Tim Horton's and she drank two cups of coffee, black. I had my French vanilla cappuccino.

"Guys don't drink that stuff," she said. "You're not turning gay or anything, are you?"

"Not to worry. Besides, isn't that kind of unfair to assume drinking French vanilla cappuccino is a gay thing for a guy to do?"

Lilly scrunched up her nose. "You are so analytical. Doesn't your brain get tired just analyzing stuff all the time?"

"Yes." I stared at the black lipstick marks Lilly had left on the white cup. It made the cup look like it had a moustache.

"So things were pretty bad with Jake?"

"Don't make me even think about it."

"Just thought you might want to talk."

"Jake is past tense."

"That's very grammatical."

"It's not about grammar, ding dong. Let's not talk about him. Or me. Let's talk about Martin. How are you?"

It was like my sister had just arrived back from an extended visit to the evil empire of Jake. I didn't quite know how to react. "I'm doing okay," I said. "Dave's been helping me a lot."

"You still do some pretty peculiar stuff."

"It's my age."

"What were you doing digging around in Mom's old flower bed at eleven o'clock the other night? That was pretty creepy. I thought maybe you had like killed someone, chopped them up into little pieces, and were burying the pieces in the garden."

"Right," I said and sipped my cappuccino. I couldn't understand why she'd make something like that up. But then sisters like mine were hard to figure out. I decided to change the subject. "I think they fired Mr. Miller."

"He was my favourite teacher in the school."

"He lost it in class after Scott Rutledge got killed."

"We should go see him."

"Can we do that?"

"Sure."

"All right. I think Darrell should come with us."

"The Egg Man?"

"He doesn't get out of the house much."

We looked Mr. Miller up in the phone book and tried calling but didn't get an answer. We picked up Darrell and went anyway. We rang and we knocked. No answer. But there was music coming from the house. Loud metal music. We waited for a lull between tunes and hammered hard on the door. It finally opened.

The heavy metal mud wrestling math teacher was home alone. He had been drinking. "Let me turn down the music," he said. "Come in."

Mr. Miller was wearing a T-shirt and sweat pants. He hadn't shaved for a couple of days. The house smelled like beer. "We came over to say hi," Lilly said.

"Things are a bit of a mess," he said apologetically, picking up some music and wrestling magazines from the sofa so we could sit down. The room looked like thieves or vandals had trashed it.

"I'm sorry to hear they kicked you out of school," Darrell blurted out.

Mr. Miller rubbed his face. "Oh, that. I've always been a little too emotional, I guess. People expect that just because I'm big and play that macho image thing that I don't hurt easily. But inside, I'm like china." He started a zigzag trek around the room, picking up crushed beer cans. He had an armload of them and looked at us like he didn't know what to do next, so

Lilly went into the kitchen and came out with a black garbage bag.

"You should recycle those," Darrell offered up.

"Yeah, Darrell, I will. I promise."

"How are you feeling?" Lilly asked Mr. Miller. I was kind of shocked that she was trying again to be helpful.

"I'm working it out, I think. I liked Scott. I just hated seeing a kid get wasted like that for no reason."

"Life sucks," Lilly said. It was a favoured motto of hers and Jake's.

"And then you freaking die," Mr. Miller said, dumping his armload of crushed beer cans into the bag.

"Are you going to appeal your dismissal?"

"I don't know. I haven't figured that out yet. Maybe I should move on from teaching."

"No way," I said.

"Why? You think that it matters? You think it does any good? Kids like me because I'm a good entertainer. That's me. Show biz. But that's all."

Lilly pulled out a pack of gum, opened it, and flipped a piece into her mouth in that way she has of doing it. Then she offered a piece to Mr. Miller. He fumbled with the wrapper and put the gum in his mouth. "The year I had you for math, I have to say you were the only teacher I had who wasn't ugly and ignorant."

"Gee thanks."

"When my sister says that, she means that, Mr. Miller."

Then Darrell cleared his throat and broke our code of silence by telling Mr. Miller and Lilly about our discussion. "Martin and I both agreed we'd change places with Scott — retroactively speaking — even though he's now dead and we're still alive."

Mr. Miller looked startled. "That's not good. In fact, it's a little scary."

"I'm still seeing the shrink," I said.

"My brother needs all the help he can get," my sister said.

"And I'm working things out in my own way," Darrell added. "I don't quite have the emotional baggage Martin has."

Mr. Miller looked halfway between stunned and bewildered. Lilly took the opportunity to say, "There are a lot of messed up kids at that school. And you understand them. Some teachers just go there to do a job and get paid. You were there to do more."

"I tried but it didn't seem to do any good."

"You probably couldn't tell if you did any good," Darrell explained, "unless you could leap ahead ten years and see those students. Then you'd know for sure if you had an impact. If we had time travel, you could do that."

"Look at me," Lilly said. "You had an impact on my life. You really did. Because of you I want to be a teacher. I'm going to go to university and get an education degree." Lilly was lying, of course, but it was a lie generated out of kindness.

Mr. Miller looked at the guitar hanging on the wall. "I was thinking about the band, a reunion, maybe going back on the road. We had some good times, you know. I used to be one hell of a guitar player."

"You still are, Mr. Miller," I said.

Stuff That May or May Not Be Important

Rollo May says that if you put a man in a cage, the first thing he does is get angry. He shouts or refuses to eat and rattles the bars of his cage. But sooner or later, he quiets down and begins to accept his fate. He gets a hollow look about him. After a while, his anger shifts to mere resentment and before long he starts to lose his feelings of rebellion. Worse yet, he eventually considers himself responsible for his predicament. After that there is not much hope, perhaps even if he is freed from the cage.

Emerso

CHAPTER FOURTEEN

Stuff

The Great Pyramid is aligned almost perfectly north-south and east-west. The guys who lined it up that way took their directions from the stars. The limestone blocks were cut from cliffs with copper saws and dragged to their destination. Most of the damn thing is granite, though, and somebody had to chip away at it with tools made of harder rocks.

The granite blocks weighed about fifty tons each and it took two million of them to make the whole structure. The blocks were dragged along on a kind of causeway affair. They say 170 men could haul one block. There would be a guy or a whole bunch of guys with pitchers of some kind of greasy stuff that would lubricate the track ahead to make things at least a little bit easier. Then the stones had to be shoved up a ramp and put into place.

The story goes that everyone was really proud of their hard-ass jobs — the block chippers, the draggers, the guys with the pitchers full of whatever pouring slimy goo to create a monument. They worked their hands to the bone and some got crushed along the way and some got really messed-up backs. A bunch of them got bit by snakes in the Nile. Some probably got depressed because they didn't believe it was all worthwhile.

It was probably better than wasting your time watching television, I'll admit, but it was like another mistake of history, a monumental waste of time.

Herodotus, who came along a mere two thousand years later, wrote about this big stone bozo of a building in the ancient city of Cheops. He did some research and learned about the male slaves who did most of the work. And where were the women? you might wonder. How come they didn't have to help drag rocks? Answer — because the slaves thought it was an honour to do the labour. Go figure. Anyway, Herodotus somehow determined what the Egyptian hackers, haulers, and greasers were eating: radishes, onions, and garlic. One whole shit-load of vegetarian food.

A hundred thousand men worked over twenty years to build the Great Pyramid of Cheops.

I'm thinking that H. must have left out some of the vittles consumed on the job. Maybe they used papyrus to make garlic and radish sandwiches or something. No mayo in those days, for sure. So you have a work crew of 170 very proud, shirtless Egyptians taking lunch break and it's as hot as the planet Venus. They chow down on their veggies and discuss how cool it is to be hauling big-ass rocks to make a tomb monument for whatever pharaoh it was. (Sorry, I can't quite remember his name, which shows you how well big rock edifices work to preserve the memory of despots.)

After lunch when they got back to shoving their prize 50,000 pounder, can you imagine the level of flatulence amongst the boys? A veritable cloud of radish, onion, and garlic farts surely must have been downright visible hovering over the scene. But there would be no vampires for sure. They didn't have any problem whatsoever with vampires in those days.

And whenever you mention pyramids, someone starts thinking aliens were involved. Like this makes a lot of sense — you invent faster-than-light-speed travel, take your shuttle to a distant planet named Earth, and then help a bunch of vegetarians move rocks that are way too big for them to be messing with in the first place. I think not.

And if these aliens showed up and saw crews of 170 men shoving a stone and simultaneously farting radish-onion-garlic farts, do you really think they would hang around? I mean, the Egyptians didn't even have pulleys. They thought they were like rocket scientists because some brilliant pharaoh pleaser had suggested the work would go easier if you employed the greaser guy with the pitcher of gobs to slime up the skid.

If the aliens showed up then, they left with ideas about better things to do.

What history teaches us, as usual, is that most of the things people spent their lives doing were a waste of time.

Napoleon showed up in 1798 at the pyramid in Cheops; he was trying to conquer the world at the time and somehow found himself in Egypt. He was impressed, of course, because he thought there were enough stones in the pyramid to build a stone wall around France. And of course, he loved the idea of some ruler who could boss around thousands if not millions of his citizens. ("Okay, you guys over there. Go shove big rocks for twenty years." "Yes, your dignity, we'd be honoured.")

Today we build Wal-Marts and video stores in shopping malls that have expected life spans of twenty years. After that, they get torn down or are turned into indoor go-cart tracks.

Emerso

I changed my mind and went to Scott's funeral. There were a lot of people there. Words were spoken. I wasn't paying much attention. Kathy stood beside me by the gravesite and when she started crying, I held her hand. I felt her hand wet with tears. I was going to say something to her and rummaged in my mind for options like, *It's okay,* or *It's going to be okay,* or *It was meant to be,* or *He's at peace now.* But I knew it was a much better policy to keep my mouth shut. Words that issued from my mouth often had unintended results.

It was a very shiny polished wooden box. My guess would be mahogany or cherry. I heard someone start laughing. It was Bill, one of the smokers. Everyone turned and looked at him as his friend Finster smacked him hard on the shoulder. "Screw you," Bill said out loud.

People scowled and then turned back to watch as the coffin was getting lowered into the ground. I was thinking about Dave just then. Dave would be expecting me to break down here — he was still waiting for me to completely freak out about my mom. He would remind me it was okay. I needed to do this thing. But today wasn't the day. I almost started laughing thanks to Bill. Laughing at funerals can be infectious and really pisses people off. I was still a little jealous of Scott even though he was in the box and someone was tossing in a shovelful of dirt on him.

Kathy was crying more and had run out of Kleenexes. I almost offered her my handkerchief until I remembered that it hadn't been washed in maybe two months. I thought about all the old dried-up snot on it and decided against it. I bet her eyes were gonna be sore after all that crying.

A minister was saying something but no one was listening. He sounded pretty sure of himself like he knew what this was all about, but I think he was just faking it. A few people tossed flowers into the grave. Scott's father poured some sand on top of the box — and I remembered that Scott had been a surfer. Finster and Bill walked up as people were beginning to leave and they dropped in a couple of cigarettes even though Scott had stopped smoking before his accident. Bill was probably thinking that if Scott had kept smoking, he might have stopped somewhere for a smoke and avoided getting into an accident and dying.

Since he died young he wouldn't ever have to be ravaged by lung cancer, so maybe he might as well have kept smoking. These are the things that go through your head when one of your classmates is being buried.

Kathy dropped a letter into the grave. I had a pretty good idea what that was all about and for a split second considered sneaking back later to steal the letter before the grave got filled in by the professional guys who fill in graves. A couple of shovelfuls of dirt is just window dressing at the ceremony.

I walked Kathy to the car where her mother was waiting. Her shoulders were kind of bent over and she looked at the ground. "Thanks for being with me," she said and got in the car.

Standing alone, I had a sudden impulse to visit my mother's grave, an easy walk from here on the other side of the cemetery. But thinking about it made me feel numb. There was no connection between her and all this. I turned my head in that direction but felt nausea in the pit of my stomach.

I looked around to see if Darrell had ever shown up but he hadn't. Mr. Cohen came over to see if I was okay. (He was still very sure I was "at risk.") "You want to go get a coffee or something?" he asked.

"I'm off caffeine. Thanks anyway," I said. Sitting down with well-meaning Mr. Cohen at a time like this would be like drill work at the dentist. I knew he was trying to be kind. "See you in school, Mr. Cohen."

"Right."

I saw Mr. Miller but he was hurrying off in the other direction. The crowd was almost gone and I started thinking about that letter Kathy had dropped on the casket. Nah, it wouldn't be right.

That's when Jake appeared.

"Kid," he said.

"Jake, what are you doing here?"

"Lilly sent me to keep an eye on you." I figured they were back together again.

"That was thoughtful of her."

"I'll walk you home."

I never liked Jake. He knew that. He never liked me. But then Jake didn't like much of anything.

"Don't feel too bad for him."

"Who?"

"Rutledge. He was a loser. Losers die young. Only the strong survive."

It was an honest appraisal coming from Jake. Jake had a kind of Darwinian view of people. Winners get rich and live without having to work; losers have to bust gut and never get anywhere and then die penniless. Scott Rutledge probably would have been one of those people to make some kind of incredible business deal just because he was charming and live happily ever after if it hadn't been for the accident.

"Are you strong?" I asked him.

"Tough. I'm tough. Takes a lot to knock me down. Maybe you could learn a thing or two from me."

"Maybe."

"You and Lilly have been through a rough time, huh?"

"You could say that."

"You got to be tough to take what you've been through," Jake said

"Thanks."

"I hate to lay this one on you now, but I think I'm going to be the one to break up with Lilly pretty soon."

"You shit."

"It's for the best. I don't know. The spark just isn't there anymore. But I've been putting it off, you know, because of your mother and all."

"Jesus, Jake, you are a friggin' humanitarian."

"I'm like that. Tough but kind deep down. I still like her. It's just that I have, as you might say, been exploring other options. You're a guy, so you understand these things. Hormones and all that. Maybe you could tell her for me."

"What do you want me to say?"

"I don't know. You're her brother. She thinks you're kind of cracked but she knows you're smart. We both think that's part of your problem."

"My problem?"

"Brainiac and all. You know. You think too much. Read too many books. Get strange ideas floating through your head."

For some reason, I was thinking about Napoleon looking on the Great Pyramid at Cheops. Napoleon calculating how the rocks in the pyramid would be taken apart and transported to become a fence around France. Jake was right about having strange thoughts.

"Jake, do you believe in reincarnation?"

"Martino, I don't believe in much of anything. That's my code to live by."

"Just suppose you and I were together in a previous life."

"What is this supposed to mean?"

"Just use your imagination. What do you think you were in a previous life?"

"I don't know. Race car driver maybe. Movie star. A guy with like a big wad of cash — nice car, fancy house, kidney-shaped swimming pool."

"Wrong. In a previous life you were a dung beetle."

Jake stopped walking. "What the hell is a dung beetle?"

"The dung beetle lives on the plains in East Africa. When elephants take a shit, the dung beetle collects the shit, rolls it to his hole in the ground where he lives, ands then eats it for the rest of the day."

Jake looked disgusted. "Dipweed. I come down here to walk you home and you tell me this. I'm hurt."

Meaning of Life

Ralph Waldo Emerson once said, "Life consists of what man is thinking of all day." He exempted women, it seems, from this definition. Maybe women actually do things and men just think. Life for most of us guys, according to Emerson, is a muddle of thoughts about primarily inconsequential things. Cyril Connolly spoke of us all spending "a life sentence in the dungeon of self."

Suppose then that you had no memory of yesterday's thoughts. The self of yesterday would disappear and you would only be the person you woke up to be today and you'd be defined by whatever goes through your head now. That might be an improvement, although there would be continuity problems. Today's self would at least be set free from the prison of yesterday's self.

Napoleon then, on his visit to Egypt, would have just leaned against the Cheops pyramid and thought it was a fine sunny day and that the rocks had a nice solid feel to them. He would have forgotten about conquering more of the world and so a whole lot of people wouldn't have suffered needlessly.

Emerso

☂ ☂ ☂

When I was a little kid I was a big fan of erasers. My mom would buy me the largest, softest eraser she could find. I wrote whole pages in pencil and then erased them until the sheet was perfectly blank again. I tried erasing newspaper stories with some success and I discovered that even the print in some books could be erased. Pen erasers were coarser and left ugly scars or even tears on the page. After a while I got the hint that some things were put down and not supposed to changed or be erased.

CHAPTER FIFTEEN

School and death seemed like a natural enough combination to me but it seemed to catch others off guard. Since nothing much of any significance ever seemed to happen in the classroom, it was a shock to our system. We'd lost Scott Rutledge and all you had to do was look at the empty seat where he usually sat to feel sad. Girls cried and left biology class. Football players got sniffly and then smashed a fist into a desk and left the room too. Teachers talked about how we all needed to "pull together."

Mr. Cohen said we should talk about it in class but that idea was squelched. Traditional shrinks (not people like Dave) came in to talk to us as we doodled in our notebooks.

The oddest thing of all was that Kathy Bringhurst started talking to me about sex. "What if a person dies and has never made love to someone she is in love with?"

"Some people believe in reincarnation," I answered matter-of-factly. I was a big fan of the idea of reincarnation but I wasn't an outright believer. I wasn't exactly a religious type, just someone who thought a lot about metaphysical stuff.

"You mean that if you don't get to do it in this life, then you will in the next?"

"Something like that."

"Have you thought a lot about sex?"

"In this life or the next?"

"Martin, you are so weird."

"You and my sister could do a chorus together."

"But I like you. Weird can be good."

"Thanks. Nobody ever quite put it that way."

"Tell me your innermost desire," Kathy insisted.

"I don't know if I can do that."

"Please. We only have a few minutes."

The bell was about to ring. We were about to depart for separate classes on opposite sides of the school. Kathy was looking at me, straight in my eyes. I think she was expecting me to say something about her — like I wanted to kiss her or make love to her. I don't know what she expected.

I closed my eyes and said the first thing that swam up in my head. "I wish I was in Norway." I opened my eyes to see the look on Kathy's face. She seemed deeply hurt and started to back away from me.

"You bastard," she screamed, then turned and ran down the hall. Other kids were watching. I just stood there wondering why I had said what I had said. It was one of those moments of both clarity and confusion. Sure, I remembered trucks and maps. I sort of knew why I wanted to be in Norway but I didn't know why I didn't say something Kathy wanted to hear. She had wanted me to say something about her. Or I could have just said nothing and kissed her. It wouldn't have been me kissing her. It would have been somebody else, but it would have been the right thing to do.

"Martin, are you going to class or are you just going to stand there in the hall?" It was the VP.

I started walking but I felt a kind of fog settling on my brain. I didn't go to class. Instead I walked to the furnace room where Declan Christmas was eating his third lunch of the day.

Declan was one of the janitors who kept the school running. He had explained to me once that he was half Aboriginal and half Irish. Both had been hungry ancestral peoples and so he packed three lunches to get him through each day.

"Tinny, boy. You all right?"

Declan had a habit of renaming everyone in the school. "You use only the last syllable and then add a 'y' at the end. Double the consonant if you have to before the 'y.' So I was Tinny (not Tiny) and Darrell was Relly, not Reily (which would have been more appropriately Irish).

The furnace room was a kind of escape pod for a number of students like me when things got screwy at school. Everyone knew this. Parents had complained, of course — there will always be parents to complain about something. This will go on until the universe collapses into itself and becomes a black hole again. Then parents will ease up.

Declan had been accused of everything and anything. Some said he was messing around with the Grade 9 girls; some said he sold drugs (because he was part Native). Some said he drank (because he was part Irish). I'd always hated people having opinions based on stereotypes. Because he was a quiet, reserved, very shy and undemanding man, one parent had even accused him of being controlled by the devil. None of it stuck. He called himself "teflon man."

"Tinny, you want half a sandwich? I'm going the vegan route for a while — no meat or dairy. But it's not half bad. I miss meat, though."

"No thanks. Just want to hang for a while. I'm hiding, really."

"Gotta hide sometime. Better to hide than run."

Things got quiet after that. The furnace was singing away and that sounded pretty good to us. I watched Declan eat his sandwich.

"Pan-fried tofu with caraway and garlic. I'm not saying it's great but I'm giving it a try. Girlfriend's a vegan so I have to at least give it a try."

"Garlic will keep away vampires."

"That's what I was thinking."

The intercom buzzed then and it was the secretary. "Declan. Clean up needed in room 235."

Declan clicked the intercom. "I'll be right down."

"Man, right after lunch. She didn't even have to say what it was. Somebody hurled in biology. I've got an instinct about these things."

And then I was alone in the furnace room as Declan rolled his mop and bucket out into the hallway. I listened to the sound of the furnace for a while and then kneeled down in front of it and looked in through the glass window so I could see the flame. I found it bright and cheerful. The flames looked like yellow leaves or flowers or something. I thought about finding Kathy when the bell rang and telling her that my "innermost desire" was to have sex with her — to make love to her — but I knew if I said it, it wouldn't be my voice. It would be someone else's. I was pretty sure I could bring myself to say it, to explain that Norway was a joke. It was a code word, I would say. Going to Norway was like "going all the way," as they used to say.

But I began to realize I was headed into some outlandish psychological territory and was bound to screw things up worse. I remembered something my English teacher had said about the semicolon: "When in doubt, leave it out." That semicolon advice seemed pretty good for now. I wouldn't mention anything to Kathy about anything. But I did have a strong impulse to reach into the furnace and pick her a handful of flowers as an apology. It was summer in there and I missed summer — the way it used to be. Instead, I tucked my hands under my legs and waited for Declan to return with news about who had puked and what it looked like.

CHAPTER SIXTEEN

"I read a quote the other day," I told Dave. "The poet Muriel Ruckeyser said the universe is made up of stories, not atoms."

"I like that. Jesus, Martin, you always floor me with something new." He tried to sound cheerful but I could tell something was actually bothering him today.

"Dave, I'm not normal," I blurted out. "There was this girl who wanted to talk about sex and I wasn't interested."

"That's not normal. But Martin, it's so you. You have your own planet in the universe of stories. It's your story. If you don't want to talk about sex with a girl, it's your privilege. She can't make you."

"I'm just not interested in sex."

"You're unique for your age."

Dave opened his green steno book and flipped some pages. "Let's see. You've ruled out smoking, anger, and sex. There's probably more. I understand that you are a kind of cerebral type kid and that makes it all the more interesting for me. What are you interested in the most?"

"I am interested in death."

"You want to talk about your mother?"

"No. I want to talk about death."

"In the abstract?"

"Yes."

"Does it seem interesting to you that you mentioned sex to me and then shifted right over to wanting to talk about death?"

"There's a connection, right?"

"Maybe. But let's not go there now."

"Dying is a wild night and a new road — Emily Dickinson."

"Skip Emily Dickinson. Go for Martin Emerson," Dave suggested.

"It's like the story thing. The story keeps going but I can't read it. It's like I bought this big fat paperback novel about my family and me. I got up to chapter seven and the pages are all blank after that. I'm the protagonist — confused but brilliant — and I keep thinking the world is full of all kinds of possibilities. But none of them are for me. I've got a really strange but interesting family, and I'm reading along to page seventy-six and I turn the page and discover there's nothing but empty pages from there to the end of the book — three hundred pages later."

"Somebody else wrote this book, right?"

"There had to be an author."

"Why doesn't he finish the book?"

"I don't know. He got tired of writing it. Or he got a real job."

"Or he died."

"He didn't die."

"Why don't you pick up the story from here? You could write it."

"I have problems with the characters. My father opted out of the story. There's not much to say about him. Lilly would get mad at me if I wrote about what she is really doing with her life."

"And you?"

"I would just wander from page to page."

"Wandering is good. How's your friend the Egg Man? Darrell?"

"Since I started ignoring him, he started his own dot-com company. People pay him to steer unaware Internet users to their websites. Has something to do with spiders or something. He doesn't know what to do with the money he's making. He says it's just a game and it doesn't feel real."

"Good ol' Darrell."

"Money is on my list of things that aren't real," I said.

"Expand the list."

"Well, nothing on television is real. Trees are real; television is not. Sex is not real; death is. I think in terms of pairs — binary coding like a computer. Lilly is real, but I don't think my father is. My mother is still real, but that's only because time is not real."

"The Buddhists think time is an illusion."

"Maybe I'm a Buddhist then."

"Go on."

"School is oddly real."

"That's good."

"After school is not. I go home, I drift, and I do homework. I wander. I argue with Lilly. And she says, 'Get real,' but I can't. Like, the other day I stole some seeds from the hardware store."

"That's good. What kind?"

"Brussels sprouts. Broccoli."

"Good vegetarian grub."

"I know. Flowers too. Delphinium, cornflower, alyssum."

"Of course."

"I wanted to get caught."

"Natch."

"Headline reads, 'Kid Caught Shoplifting Packets of Seeds.' I wanted the experience of being questioned."

Dave put on the mock voice for me, turned his desk lamp to shine in my face. "Why'd you steal the seeds, kid? 'Fess up."

"I dunno. But I walked out of the store cool as a cucumber sandwich."

"Then what?"

"I went home," I lied. I didn't know why I felt like I had to lie to Dave. I couldn't remember what I did after I left the store. Maybe it wasn't important. Maybe I goofed around and then went home. But it was like turning the page again in the novel and the next page was blank.

"What did you do with the seeds? Did you plant them?"

"Maybe." But I couldn't remember what I did with the seeds. Maybe they were in my room.

"Let me try to pull this together today. Girl wants to talk about sex and you let her down. You hang out with the janitor in the furnace room and see flowers in the fire. Then you steal some seeds from a store. We could sell the film rights to this, you know."

I laughed. Dave was such a crazy guy. But he still looked troubled about something that didn't have anything to do with me.

Then came the big confession.

"Martin, I've got to tell you something that no one else around here knows. I know I shouldn't do this. But I've been realizing that if I don't tell someone, I'm going to need some kind of therapy myself."

"You gonna tell me you're gay? If that's it, it's no big deal."

"No, I wish it was that simple."

"Let me guess. You were Hitler in a previous incarnation."

"Don't think so."

"Okay, I'll shut up. What's up, doc?"

"I don't think I'm very good at what I do. I'm a failure. See those diplomas on the wall?"

"Sure."

"They don't mean a thing. It's not like they're fake. It's just that they seem artificial. I know the textbook stuff. I just don't think much of it works. I don't ever seem to really cure anyone."

I stared at the diplomas and put a hand in my pocket, discovered that there were some loose seeds in there. The universe made up of stories. Things are not always as they appear to be. Dave had been on my list of things that were real. Dave: real. Me: not real.

Dave kept talking, but I wasn't paying close attention. I suddenly realized that I should have kissed Kathy there in the hallway. I should have told her that was my innermost desire. I should have proven to her that I was as much alive as Scott Rutledge was dead. Instead, I opted for flowers in a furnace.

"I wouldn't keep up the facade," Dave went on, "except for the fact that my intentions are good. I want to help people. That's why I got into this profession in the first place."

"Stick with it. Maybe your therapy will work one day. I think you're doing the best you can with me."

"You're not shocked and appalled."

"I react slowly to things as you know. Maybe it will hit me later."

"I shouldn't have unloaded this on you of all people. You may want to cancel your sessions."

"I'd rather keep going. A guy misses an opportunity to kiss a beautiful girl, he's got to have problems, don't you think?"

"Martin, we all have problems, believe me. Some of us just create bigger ones than others."

"Dave. Don't tell your other patients about your doubts. They may not understand you the way I do. You're good at what you do. People need you. That makes it pretty real, don't you think?"

"Easy for you to say."

"Want my advice?" I asked.

"Shoot."

"Take up smoking."

When I walked outside, I was surprised. It was spring. I'd missed it sneaking up on us. I noticed flowers about to happen and buds on trees. I wondered if my father knew it was spring. I wondered if he could see it happening around him.

The universe was full of stories, not atoms.

Advice

Roll with the unexpected. If scientists discover that the moon is truly made out of green cheese, don't be overly surprised.

Don't get angry if things appear one way and are actually another. The world stands aside to let you pass if you know where you're going. It may, however, be a disappointment when you get there. Don't be afraid to change roads or trains or whatever form of transportation works for you. Don't use a surfboard for a bicycle or skis on paved roads. When you are walking, realize that while you are in motion, one foot is almost always off the ground or about to be. Confusion is prior to enlightenment, says some ancient Chinese dude whose name I can't remember.

Missed opportunities haunt you till the end of your days, but created opportunities are the only way to make up for the loss.

Sorry, folks, I was in one of those moods. Take your pick of the above. But again, I remind you, if you are spending a lot of time hanging out in my chat room — or anybody's chat room — get out of the house and see if the planet is still okay. All major damage to the planet should be reported to the police. Try to avoid walking on spiders and flowers and keep your eyes out for injured animals.

And if anyone knows how to recover from being a stupid ass in front of someone you care for, leave it on the notice board. It's not for me, but someone I know.

Emerso

CHAPTER SEVENTEEN

Opinions

"All knowledge and all beliefs consist of judgements."

A. Wolf,
Textbook of Logic

I couldn't decide if I was the one who should break the bad/good news about Jake to my sister. Darrell's idea is that if you want to forget about something and just put it out of your brain you just "delete the file." Darrell did not show up for Scott Rutledge's funeral because he said he was close to breaking into the

Microsoft data bank or possibly the Pentagon. His back-up plan was to mess with Merrill Lynch.

"Don't worry, Martin, I follow the prime directive of non-interference. I just want to get inside, see if I can do it. I will slip in and then slide out, undetected. Give myself a merit badge, metaphorically speaking, and then move on."

Darrell didn't invent new viruses or worms. "Worms are for assholes that hold grudges," he said. "And viruses are old and pointless. No sense of humour. 'A Man's reach should exceed his grasp.'" Like me, Darrell had a way of holding old quotes in his head.

"Only one link in the chain of destiny can be handled at a time," I reminded him. Darrell was going to have to look that one up.

He and I had discussed a computer variation of a positive virus, something that infected your computer and improved your life. We'd argued at length as to what it might do — not exactly how; that's Darrell's department.

What could we do by way of your e-mail that could truly improve your life?

We were an old-fashioned couple of nerdlings in that we came to the conclusion (again) that you had to earn something in order for it to be of value. So all we could hand out were tools. And of course that was what my site was all about. I was offering my humble advice, tidbits of logic and insight for curious brains.

The funeral had left me feeling like I'd just been to a funeral. Talking with Jake made me feel worse. Lilly was going to feel even more terrible when Jake dumped her next time instead of her dumping him. I wouldn't know what to do for her.

I decided I would take the oblique approach. I would unload the problem on my father (of all people) and see if he could react. A man asleep for so many days and months is bound to wake up sometime. I missed my father almost as much as I missed my mother. Even though he was there in the house. The Invisible Man had put his home life on permanent hold. He was part of the casualty count.

I was surrounded by body bags. Scott, for sure. Man down. For good. Mr. Miller, too. And my father. And Kathy, in a kind of Emily Dickinsonian doomed-love-struck cloud.

Dogs barked as I passed one house after another. Pekingese, poodle. Lab. Great Dane. Newfoundland dog. All aliens transported here from other planets to find host humans who would feed and shelter them. Intergalactic scam number thirty-seven. Fair enough trade.

Back to the body count. Darrell, the fragile egg that he was, could get himself into deep trouble. Someone would crack his safety shell. He was messing with the big boys. Bill Gates was going to find out, or the CIA or someone. Then he'd have to explain that his intentions were pure. "All rising to great places is by a winding stair," as Sir Francis Bacon would say.

Dave was headed for a footstep into a major psychological cow pie. I was wishing he hadn't told me about his doubts. Maybe he was just making that part up. Rorschach test kind of thing. And now Lilly. About to be crushed. What would she pierce next?

It was five-thirty by the time I walked up the driveway. The van was parked in the usual place. I touched the side of it as I walked by, wondering why I always had a certain kind of "feeling" each time the van was there.

My father was in the kitchen, tie off, stir-frying vegetables. The house smelled of onions, garlic, and yes, even radishes. Men about to build pyramids or what?

Into the stir-fry, the old man threw a red slab of steak. He looked at me guiltily.

"Smell of red meat in the house used to really bother your mother, but she didn't complain."

"Mom wasn't a whiner."

"Truly."

"Dad. How was your day?" Expecting mono or dual syllables at most.

"It sucks to be me," he said, flipping the steak.

"Why don't you quit?"

"And do what?"

"Start your own business."

"I'm too old for that. I've got a path; just need to stick to it. Retire someday."

"You're thinking about retirement? No way."

He stood back from the stove; looked up at the ceiling. "Your mother and I started out creative. She painted, I wrote. Art and literature. You saw her stuff from art school. She was out there. Really out there in her own territory. Extraordinary. I tried to keep up. I wrote poetry."

"You wrote poetry?"

"Bad poetry, but poetry. I wanted to be a poet. Grew a little beard, had a way of standing and looking off into space. Thinking poetic thoughts. I read my poetry out loud to her at night by flashlight beneath the stars."

"I knew you two did some weird stuff before Lilly and me came into the picture." Something about the smell of meat frying in the kitchen and my father talking to me in full sentences made me feel like it was a big moment. We were connecting in a way that hadn't happened in a long while.

"I should never have been lured into advertising. I followed the money instead of my gut instinct."

"What did your gut instinct say?"

"Alaska. It said, go to Alaska."

"That's what you and Mom always talked about, but I didn't think you really wanted us to do it. It was just a game, yeah?"

"Yes and no."

Dad stabbed the steak with a fork and held it up in the air.

"Want some?"

"Shall I call Lilly?"

"Sure."

"Jake told me he's breaking up with Lilly."

"Jake is scum. She's better off."

"She's still going to be devastated."

"What do we do?"

"I was hoping you had an idea."

"Jesus."

I knocked on Lilly's door and told her about supper.

"We never eat together."

"Dad cooked stir-fry and steak."

"What's the occasion?"

"He thinks his job sucks. So he decided to cook a steak."

"Okay."

The three of us sat at the kitchen table. Lilly opened a can of Clamato juice and poured a big glass, then added a hefty dose of Tabasco sauce. My father started to talk and Lilly looked at me with a "what is going on here?" stare.

"So now they have me writing ad copy for Odor Eaters. This is what it comes down to. One day you're sitting under a tall cedar tree writing poetry, and the next you're writing about foot odour."

"Dad, get a grip," Lilly said. "People have stinky feet. They need the information you provide so they know what to buy to stop the stink."

"Think of it as a public service," I added. I liked everything about my sister and I trying to cheer him up.

"I'm not even that good at what I do," he went on. "I could write something brilliant if I wanted to, but what they want is something predictable."

"You work for an ad agency. What did you expect?"

"I don't know. I expected more."

"Jake says that he thinks advertising has replaced religion," Lilly said. "He doesn't think that's so bad."

My dad looked at me. Lilly didn't have a clue that Jake was about to dump her. My father didn't say anything, but I couldn't keep my mouth shut. "Jake has the IQ of a foot fungus," I said, keeping with the foot and mouth theme of dinner.

"Oh, that's so sweet," Lilly said, back to her old sarcastic self.

Dad was studying a piece of steak on the end of his fork. His mind was at work — making connections I couldn't quite begin to fathom.

"That does it," he said. "We're going to Alaska."

And we finished the meal in silence. But it wasn't the silence usually accompanying any family encounter with the Invisible Man. It was different. Maybe the toxins in the red meat had triggered some long-dormant endorphins that made my father react thus. But it was like he had returned from the dead.

CHAPTER EIGHTEEN

Meaning of Life

The more I know, the less I understand. I think the best any of us can do is keep on living. The world is unfair and unjust as I have discovered and some of you have as well. Admit it now and let it be part of you but don't let it destroy you, make you cynical, or turn you into an asshole.

Wait for weird interesting shit to happen. It will and you should revel in it. But you have to keep your eyes open. Most people you and I know have their eyes closed even while they are awake. If you are bored with everything, it's you. It's not the world. If you're angry at everything, it probably is the fault of the world, not you. You are human; you expect more than that. So you should be good and pissed off.

I predict that something will happen to you in the next twenty-four hours that will be extraordinary. I know this because I understand the people who come to Emerso.com. You are here because you expect something more. You are not looking up porno sites, playing silly, violent games, or watching movie stars being interviewed. You have a hunch that life is about to bite you on the ass. That's why you are here.

I am not just messing with your mind for fun. I know some stuff and what I know is that something WILL happen to you in the next twenty-four hours. It will change your life if you let it. You might miss it, however, so if you do, it's your fault, not mine. This THING may even appear to be negative at first until you realize the significance. It can come from within or it can be something that happens to you. I don't know the details. I just know it will happen. You can post your experience on the bulletin board of this site.

I'm not going to explain to you why this event will happen to you now but, you'll have to trust me. As most of you know, I haven't steered you wrong before. Like I said, I'm not just messing with your head. You've got television and teachers and presidents for that. This is real. I'm not telling you this because of any planetary alignment or any of that astrological sort of thing. I don't know what Jupiter is doing right now and I don't particularly care.

But I do care about you. And you've trusted me before. If you believe that something extraordinary will happen, send me an e-mail to the site and I'll keep tabs on what's going on. But I won't offer more advice. You'll have to figure the rest out for yourselves. You're on your own, as you should be, cowboys and cowgirls.

Like Roy Rogers often said to Dale Evans, "Happy Trails to you."

Emerso

Well, we didn't pack up and go to Alaska right then, like Dad said. He went back to writing ad copy about foot odour. And I put off telling Lilly about rat-face Jake.

At school I started to get scared about what I had posted on Emerso. I knew I had a big audience. I knew my "followers" sometimes took me way too seriously. What if people expected too much? What if they did something stupid and got hurt looking for "something extraordinary." I knew it was a game, a suggestion game, but, like I told them, I wasn't just messing with their minds. I was trying to open eyes. When I wrote for Emerso, I always felt sure of what I was saying — or at least I felt honest. At the heart of the honesty was this core of something mythical. The myth of Emerso the Wise. Some people out there, according to my fan mail, really needed Emerso. And so did I. Maybe when I was older, Emerso and I would be one and the same.

The ghost of Scott Rutledge was still haunting the school. I could see the effect everywhere in the faces of the sad girls at school. Teachers droned on about who knows what. I kept seeing my own reflection in the shiny doors of lockers. Darrell found me by the water fountain. I was now in the habit of drinking at least three litres of water a day.

"You still believe water makes you smarter?" he asked.

"Yes. It irrigates the brain cells."

"Good theory. But the water moves in and it moves out quickly."

"Maybe man's purpose is to act as a water transportation system. You drink it at point A and piss it out at point B."

"Yeah, but all you're doing is taking it from the pipe here in the hallway and then moving it to the urinal in the boy's room across from Ms. Vogler's classroom. Not much of an accomplishment."

"Distance is relative," I said.

"Isn't everything?"

"But suppose I quaffed a gallon or so here," I theorized, "got on a plane and held it in until I got to, say, Kuala Lumpur. That would be major liquid displacement. If a million or so people did that each day for a month, it could lead to climate change. That would be something to brag about."

"What about Scott? He ate a bunch of cheeseburgers and french fries, added some other chemicals, and had this big package of molecules that he delivered back to the earth. Was that what he was here for?"

"Maybe that was all there was to it, Darrell. Maybe that was okay."

The Egg Man's eyes rolled. "Metaphysics is not my domain, remember. I just want to be a cyborg someday and avoid the continuation of the whole organic journey."

"You may have to settle for being a brain in a vat."

"Better than being six feet under."

I drank some more water. "Too much chlorine."

"I slipped into Microsoft HQ," Darrell said matter-of-factly. "The guys running their system are old. Nearly thirty, I'd guess. They're losing their edge. Oh, and I saw what you posted on your site. I'm a bit of an agnostic on your prognostics. So far, I got an A on a quiz, my pen ran out of ink, I discussed bio-water transport with my best friend — but the heavens have not opened to reveal the face of God."

"Has it been twenty-four hours yet?"

"No."

"Then hang in and wait."

We were late for class. But everybody was breaking rules today. The smokers were cutting out from school, headed towards what was left of the woods. I saw Mr. Cohen turn and pretend he didn't see. Bill nodded and fingered the cigarette pack in his pocket as he walked by me.

"Nicotine transport systems," Darrell said.

As I watched the smokers exit from the dark hallway out into the bright light of the afternoon, their silhouettes looked like characters in a science fiction movie passing into another dimension.

"What if this is as good as it gets?"

"Who are you? Jack Nicholson?"

"I got over three hundred e-mails from people who believe something amazing is going to happen today."

"They believed in you, man."

"I wish I was like them. I wish I could read some words on the Internet and believe."

"But you the man. You are the great Emerso with all the answers. Or at least theories. You sure you don't want me to add movie music to your site? For effect."

"No. Let's keep it pure."

"Untainted. But don't lose the art. The images are great."

I had almost forgotten about the paintings we had put up on the site. My mother's art, even the unfinished ones. Other worlds. Soft dreamy places. Better places.

I saw Jake headed towards the same door that the smokers had used for an exit. I waved Darrell away and ran to catch up with him. He looked really ticked off.

"I thought I told you to talk to her, you little jerk."

"I was meaning to."

"But what, you had something more important to do?"

"She knows?"

"Now she knows, but it was all messed up because I thought she already knew. No one should ever trust you to deliver a message." He left and slammed the door in my face.

Lilly would be devastated. I needed to find her.

I checked the math class she was supposed to be in, peering in through he window, but she wasn't there.

Only one place for Lilly to go when sorrow struck: the mall.

Halfway there I had to pee real bad, which prompted me to use the washroom at the Burger King. Burger King and McDonald's had always been on my mother's boycott list because hamburgers and vegetarians didn't mix well. I finished my morning's water transport obligations and was headed back outside. Something about going from the air-conditioned Burger King out into the warm springtime midday sun made me feel dizzy. I sat down on a thin strip of grass and dandelions and had this weird feeling that I was looking down at myself from above. It only lasted a twelfth of a second; I closed my eyes and saw purple splotches and then something else kicked in. I was in the landscape of one of my mother's paintings. And I was driving down a forest road. I knew how to drive — as if I'd been doing it for a long time.

When I opened my eyes I was still in front of Burger King. I was a long way from wherever I'd been but I wanted to go back inside my mother's painting. I wanted to be there, in that landscape, driving our old van. I wanted it so badly that it hurt like a pain inside my chest. I must have looked pretty strange, like a kid on drugs or something, because a couple of women were staring at me.

"Sorry, just a little flatulence," I said. "Red meat'll do that to you. I wouldn't eat here if I were you."

I heard some kind of soft hum in my ears as I got up and walked towards the mall. I also thought I was seeing auras around things. The mailbox had a blue one and a Pekingese dog on a leash had a yellow one. The owner, an elderly man with coke bottle glasses, had a great halo of green around him. Cars had silver auras and even the sidewalk had a kind of light emanating from it. The mall up ahead had no aura at all.

I found Lilly in the process of getting her tongue pierced at the hair/beauty place. The guy was pushing a large needle straight through her tongue and she looked like she was in pain.

I sat down in a chair and she saw me. She glared in my direction but couldn't talk because the needle was still through her tongue. The receptionist asked me if she could help me, and, while I was staring at my sister, I asked, "Do you do brain piercing? I'd really like to put a ring through my brain."

CHAPTER NINETEEN

In the hallway just outside the piercing parlour I sat down
on the floor and waited for Lilly while people walked by.
Some of them stared at me as if I had a nuclear bomb
right there and I was preparing to do something mean.
This is why people should not be allowed to carry knives,
handguns, stink bombs, or thermonuclear devices. I'm
convinced of it. Anger should be turned into something
creative, not destructive, if at all possible, and if that
doesn't work, do what my father does and take a nap.

I poked my head back into the salon and saw that
Lilly was finished so I went back in. "Let's call Dad,"
she said to me right away. "We should go to Alaska
today." Behind her, two young women were getting
their hair dyed, one Jell-O green, one pink.

Lilly looked mad at somebody and it wasn't hard to
understand why. I'm sure she was in pain. She glared at

me. As if I was the source of the pain. I looked up. For some reason, the fluorescent lights buzzing above my head made me angry too. I decided to look up the guy who invented fluorescent lights and say nasty things about him on my website. Lilly paid for the piercing. She now had a small silver stud in the middle of her tongue. I could think of a million reasons why a person would not want to have such a thing but I would not use my own tongue to utter negative thoughts.

"Jake is not much more than salamander shit," I said as we walked through the mall.

"Jake thinks I'm not good enough for him," Lilly said. "Why didn't you tell me?"

"It was just bad timing. You should have called it quits after you dumped him before."

"I was in love with the rat. I think I still am."

"The man has clam mucous for a brain. His heart is a small little weasel turd. You are better off without him."

Lilly stopped and turned, looked at me, then up at the ceiling of the mall where banners hung down in blue and red. "Jake was a kind of anchor for me, Martin. But it was more than that. You probably wouldn't understand."

"I understand that you feel hurt."

Lilly looked at me hard, angry with me again. "Martin, you don't know anything about pain. You didn't cry when Mom died. You never show any emotion. You don't know."

I said nothing. I didn't know what to say about what I did or didn't know.

"You're lucky, you know," she added. "I want to be like you. Teach me, Martin. This is your gift to the world. Teach us all to feel no pain." Lilly opened her mouth and touched the silver ball in the centre of her tongue. It hurt, I could tell.

"I'll buy you a coffee."

"I'm not supposed to drink or eat anything for a while."

"What do you want to do?"

"I'm quitting school."

"You've said that before."

"I'm serious this time."

"I'll quit with you," I said. "Maybe we can do home schooling together."

Lilly tried to laugh but that hurt too. Life seemed to be full of pain for her. Her point about life being painful for everyone but me was making me feel pretty uncomfortable inside. Mr. Numb. Emotions all sealed up inside, vacuum packed.

We were walking across the mall parking lot. I looked up at the sun and then saw the purple splotches again, followed by the auras. Lilly's aura was red. Anger and pain. I looked at my hand — no aura. Just like the mall. Maybe I was just a ghost. A product of Lilly's imagination.

Lilly tore open her purse, yanked out her little cellphone and punched in a phone number. "Dad? I want to go to Alaska. I want to go to Alaska now."

I remember my mother getting angry with me once when I was quite small. I had a hammer and I was cracking open the shells of several large snails in her garden. Why I remember this when other territory is blank, I don't know. But I do.

I enjoyed the sound made by my hammer smashing on the shells of the poor snails, and somehow my brain had not made connection to the fact that I was killing the living thing inside. I think it was because I honestly didn't know that things could die. Or if I was intrinsically aware of this fact, I kept it buried in some secret place that had no relation to my day-to-day life.

I had massacred at least a dozen snails when my mother came on the scene. She tore the hammer out of my hand and threw it across the yard. Then she glowered at me, much as Lilly glared at me when I showed up during the tongue-piercing. Lilly had inherited my mother's tiny arsenal of anger and done ambitious things with it during her formative and teenage years.

I think my mother almost spanked me for killing the snails but she didn't follow through. Instead, she yelled at me in words that I did not understand back then. It was the tone of voice that mattered. I'm sure the lesson had to do with preserving life and never harming living things — words that would be heard again as I grew older, words of wisdom, sometimes coupled with tirades against corporations and greed and government and bastards who cut down trees with chainsaws.

There I sat guiltily amidst the carcasses of snails — a serial snail killer in my mother's own garden. An ugly scene for sure. My mother kneeled down and gathered up the demolished snails, picked up her weeding fork and made a small mass grave for them. I began to cry as she buried them. Then she cried.

Next, my mother picked me up and sat me down with her in the backyard hammock and we swung back and forth in a warm morning breeze.

A few days later may father ran over the hammer in the yard with the lawn mower and it wrecked the blade. He wanted to know how in blazes the hammer ended up in the grass, and my mother said it was her fault but she didn't tell the whole story.

Guilt is a powerful educational tool and I dared not kill a thing after that. I hadn't really thought snail shells had living things inside, I suppose, so I didn't know what else might be alive. I stopped throwing stones, for example. And I had come to the even odder conclusion that dust was alive. I had a lot of dust under my bed and nobody had ever cleaned up under there that I knew of so I thought of all that dust as alive and growing under my bed. My mother was in my room once and said, "Martin, you sure have a lot of dust under your bed. We'll have to do something about that."

I was proud of the dust and went on living in harmony with it there in my room. As far as I know, no one ever did vacuum it up or anything and I slept peacefully at night feeling that I was protecting that small kingdom of living, if not sentient, dust.

I don't think my mother knew about my thoughts on dust. She didn't fully forgive me for snail smashing until later that summer while I was playing with my trucks, driving to Kansas, Utah, and on to Mongolia, when she saw a mosquito biting me on the cheek. I had trained myself not to swat bugs that were biting me. It was quite a discipline but I would let bugs bite if it was in their nature. So this one mosquito got quite a bellyful of my youthful blood as I held my breath and waited for it to fly off. My mother saw this and finally came towards me as the blood-bloated mosquito flew away of its own accord. She looked in my eyes and understood what I was thinking.

I received an honorary hug and a kiss on my bloody cheek.

Down the street from us was a kind of park — just a field, really, owned by the town — where tall grasses grew. In the centre of the field was a large oak tree. Teenagers sat under the tree at night, smoked dope and did other things that I can only guess at. In the day-time, the tree pretty much had the field to itself.

My mother would do paintings of the tree but each painting was different and she always added things like mountains or huge swooping birds or turned the one tree into a jungle. She carried an easel and canvas and a palette of watercolours, sometimes acrylics — and sometimes those paints made from egg yolks and pigment known as tempera — to the mid-dle of the field where she went into a kind of trance-like state as she painted one tree into an entire imag-inary world of beauty. On occasion, I would go hang out with my mother and study ants or spiders while she painted.

Why I climbed the tree that particular day, I don't know, but I had spent much of my summer at ground level with trucks and ants and things of the earth. Some enterprising youth before me had nailed a couple of small boards onto the back of the tree — on the side my mother could not see. I found myself climbing up into that old oak tree and feeling very brave and intelligent. One branch led to the next until I was high up into the lofty places that a tree can take a boy. There were birds and green leaves blocking the sun and it was an altogether satisfying place to be.

My mother was probably looking straight at the tree while I climbed, but the leafy arms of oak blocked me from view. I found a comfortable branch, positioned myself, and sat. I began to talk to the tree — that seemed like the appropriate thing to do — telling the tree it was my friend and that if it wanted to, I could drive it in my truck to Norway or South Carolina or wherever it wanted to go.

But the tree did not want to go anywhere. It had a jovial old man kind of personality — cheerful, tolerant, and enduring. It swished the leaves at the end of its branches and seemed inclined to be my friend for the day.

And then I looked down.

The tree had somehow tricked me and taken me way up into the sky. Even though I had climbed what seemed an easy ladder of natural branches, there appeared to be no way down from these lofty heights. When the wind blew, the leaves opened up and I could see my mother, painting away at her easel. I could tell that she had been sitting in the sun too long and was starting to turn a little red. I called out, but it seemed like my voice was swallowed up by the leafy canopy and I wondered why the tree had tricked me into such a dangerous situation.

I was paralyzed with fear over the height and I decided I could not attempt descent. I yelled for help several times until my mother was awakened from her artistic swoon and came searching for the disembodied voice of her son.

The rescue was not easy for her as she hugged me to her with one strong arm, moving us downward from branch to branch as we found our way back to earth. I remember her breathing — shallow and rapid and finally followed by a great heave of relief when she set me down into the grass. But I do not remember any words.

When I saw the painting for the first time, I saw a tree that seemed to be illuminated from within. In the background were buildings — pagodas and strange Oriental architecture — and in the foreground was a river with women along the banks and water the colour of dark tea.

The day the men arrived with chainsaws to cut down the tree, my mother was on hand to protest. She had a sign and she shouted at the men, but it was the tail-end of her futile battle to save the tree. My father, somewhat sheepishly, added his voice to what my mother had to say, but the starting of three chainsaws at once drowned it out. The field was to be turned into several ballfields for little league baseball. Most everyone in the town thought baseball was more important than one old oak tree.

A photograph of my mother had been in the paper showing her arguing with the mayor and a man in a hard hat. She garnered a reputation as a tree hugger and a crazy woman and she wore that reputation as if it was the uniform of a small ambitious army of one.

I never played baseball on that field, but sometimes in the early morning, before joggers or baseball players would come to the park, my mother would go back to the field, set up her easel, and stare at the spot where the tree used to be. And she'd paint her luminous landscapes, erasing the fences and the billboards and the backstops in favour of a softer, more colourful rendering of another level of reality that continued to live on in my mother's imagination.

CHAPTER TWENTY

✦ ✦ ✦

Stuff That May or May Not Be Important

Friederich Wilhelm Nietzsche thought people acted too much like slaves to the institutions of government and religion. He died in 1900 with only one foot in the twentieth century. He thought there should be certain extraordinary individuals, super-men, who were above the common mass of dopes. These god-like individuals could assert their will and attract others to share the vision and do great things — reshape the world as we know it.

Nietzsche was also a great lover of sausage. He was a true meat eater, but then that came with the smorgasbord of the fatty German diet. He wrote about greatness and super-individuals after eating a lot of sausage. I don't know if there is a connection. He thought most of us were a bunch of wimpy nincompoops, although that was not the term he used. Nietzsche had some good ideas, or at least he had a way of getting people to think outside of the box.

Adolph Hitler was eleven years old the year Nietzsche died. I don't know much about what Hitler did as a boy. Maybe he played with toy soldiers and had toy military trucks that he pretended to drive to Norway and Africa. I know that Hitler liked flowers, too. He even painted, which seems very odd when you think about it.

Unfortunately for the world, Hitler read what Nietzsche had to say about the so-called "will to power" and Adolph really liked what he read. He stirred Nietzsche's notions around with a bunch of other stuff rattling around in his European brain and ended up doing what we all know he did. If Hitler had just been a lazy daydreamer or a plain no-good schmuck who said rude things to people in the beer halls of Munich, things wouldn't have been so bad for the world. But some people aren't satisfied to leave things the way they are.

Emerso

"What's this all about?" my father asked after he pulled the van to a stop in front of the mall. The van had a faint orange aura that surprised me because the van itself was forest green.

My father had a soft yellow halo, but I was starting to wish the weird visual stuff would go away. I was getting a headache.

"I think we should just leave — the three of us, before it's too late," Lilly said.

My father loosened his tie and sat down on the curb. "I left a meeting with a client. We were discussing demographics. I was explaining that our ideal target was a forty-year-old male who had a high-stress job and worried about money, family, and foot odour in that order. This is what I'm reduced to."

"Another good reason to drive to Alaska," Lilly added.

My father blinked and looked up at the sky. He seemed truly confused but he was no longer the Invisible Man.

"I haven't been helping you kids, I know. All I can do is keep myself going, one meaningless day after the next."

"We all miss her," Lilly said.

"I keep waiting for one morning to be different," my dad said. "I keep waiting to wake up and feel something less terrible than what it felt like yesterday. But it doesn't happen."

"Let's just get in he van and drive," Lilly said.

"I'm okay with that," I said. There was this big fog bank forming in the back of my brain. I didn't know what it was about. The whole scene seemed unreal to me, like I was not here but watching these two people in a movie. I couldn't quite comprehend why my father was saying he had felt terrible day after day. It never once showed on his empty face each morning.

"I don't think it's the right thing to do," my dad said, and then he looked at me, noticed something about me.

"You okay, Martin?"

But Martin was sitting in the audience somewhere. He didn't have any lines in the script. Martin felt like he didn't fully understand what they were talking about. Who exactly was it they missed so badly? Who was it that was gone?

"Martin?"

"Yeah, I'm okay. I was just thinking about something else."

"Lilly, I'm a little worried about Martin."

"Don't worry about me," I said. "I want to go to Alaska, too. I think it's the right thing to do."

"I'm going to see if Dave can see Martin before we take off. I want to be sure this is the right thing to do." He pulled out his cellphone and made the call.

"It's all set. Dave can see you in fifteen minutes. He said he wanted to talk to you anyway. Let's go."

"Wait," Lilly said. She looked at me and then at my dad. "Let Martin drive."

"What?" he asked.

"Let Martin drive."

"He doesn't know how," my father said.

I couldn't understand why she was doing this.

Lilly took the keys from my father and handed them to me. "Drive, Martin."

CHAPTER TWENTY-ONE

My father sat in the seat beside me and said, "Put on your seat belt. You too, Lilly."

I started the engine and checked the mirrors. Then I drove out of the mall parking lot, heading for Dave's office. No one in the car said a word or doubted my driving ability. The town looked different from behind the wheel. But I seemed to know how to handle the traffic just fine. I took my time, stopping for yellow lights — overly cautious. I passed the corner where Scott's brother had dumped his bike, the place Scott had been killed in the accident. I kept my eyes on the road but when I checked the rear-view mirror, there was Lilly, staring at me. We had to drive by our house without stopping and that seemed very surreal — as if some other family lived there, as if everything was normal inside that home. I noticed how overgrown the front yard was with the high grass and weeds in the flower beds. No one said a word and I just kept driving.

I parked in front of Dave's home office. I handed the keys to my father but couldn't begin to explain anything about how I had learned to drive.

"I think I want to go in by myself," I said.

"We'll wait out here," my father said. "Lilly and I have some catching up to do."

Dave pretended to be casual. "Your father says you are all driving to Alaska. They have grizzly bears up there, you know."

"It's not the grizzly bears I'm afraid of."

"Something else?"

"Well, me, for starters."

"Courage imperils life; fear protects it. I got that from somewhere."

"I don't know what I'm protecting."

"You are probably trying to protect you. That's the way it usually works. Look, if this is serious, maybe I need to get you connected with someone with, um, more experience in these things than me."

"I'm not letting you off that easy. Besides, I trust you."

"Trust is a big word."

"Well, right now I don't trust myself and I need someone to trust. My family is a little confused and I'm seeing halos around people so I'm gonna trust you to tell me I'm not crazy."

"You're not crazy. What kind of halos?"

"I can see colour around people. It kind of vibrates or shimmers. Yours is yellow."

"Does that mean I'm a coward?"

"I don't know what it means. But it's only the tip of the iceberg."

"But we're not on the *Titanic*. You are seeing energy fields. Some people can do that. Auras. Might be your eyes playing tricks or might be you really do see them. When did this start?"

"When I walked out of Burger King."

"Something they put on your Whopper?"

"I didn't eat anything. But it's not the auras that bother me. There's more."

"That's what I'm here for."

"I drove here. Me. I drove the van. I drove like I've been driving for a long time. I didn't make any mistakes. Dave, I don't drive. I've never driven before. But Lilly somehow knew I could drive."

Dave could see that I was scared. And I was scared. There was more to it, but I didn't know what else there was. I wished I were sitting back in school, bored out of my skull in that usually warm, fuzzy place, listening to a teacher drone on about something I wasn't interested in.

"Want me to invite Lilly and your dad in?"

"No. I think I scared my Dad. Lilly knows something but she isn't talking."

"Martin. Look at it this way for starters. Everyone has been worrying about you because you've been acting so normal since…"

"Since she died?"

"Yes. Now you have this sort of odd streak going for you and you don't feel normal, right?"

"Dave, I know this is the sort of shrink logic you are famous for, but now that I'm not normal, I think I liked it the other way. Because it was safe."

"Maybe safe is for losers, Martin. So what's the worst-case scenario you can think of for the auras and the driving?"

"I don't know. I was abducted by aliens and they gave me some kind of extra visual sense and they taught me how to drive for some reason."

"Maybe they needed a chauffeur."

I heaved a sigh. "I wish it was that simple."

"You're suggesting it is not."

"Right."

"Let's ask Lilly what she knows."

"Not yet. I feel like I have to get it from me first. I'm missing some pieces of the puzzle. Lots of them.

Can you hypnotize me?"

"Sure, but aren't you afraid I'll make you act like a chicken?"

"No. I trust you."

It was a dark night, frost on the grass, a half moon. I was sitting in my room looking at one of my mother's landscape paintings. Everything had a glow to it: the clouds, the trees, and the mountains in the background. I couldn't bring myself to go to bed because I knew I wouldn't be able to sleep.

I closed my eyes and tried to remember what my mother looked like, but it seemed impossible.

Then my brain seemed to suddenly shut down and when it fired up again, I was driving our van down the street. I was nervous and oversensitive to everything, ready to slam on the brakes if anything surprised me, but I knew where I was going and what I was doing.

I drove straight there, parked, and walked across the grass. I had forgotten to put on a jacket and I was cold. I could see my breath. There was no wind. No sound except for a few dogs barking somewhere. I wasn't scared.

The marble was smooth and cold to the touch and I held my hand on it for a long time, then moved my cheek to it and felt how the cold was transferred. I kneeled down on the grass and cleared the frost from over the grave. I knew where I was and even why I was there. I started talking to her and at first the sound of my own voice scared me.

No one else was around, although I didn't seem to care if anyone found me there. I knew it was where I had to be. I didn't tell her how much I loved her or how much I missed her. I talked about me. I told her about school, about Kathy Bringhurst. I told her about my website, about Darrell still trying to hack into Microsoft. I told her about what a jerk Jake was.

And then I started talking about surprise quizzes. Suppose your teacher tells you there's going to be a surprise quiz on one of the next five days. If you get to day four and it hasn't happened, then it can't happen on day five because it's predictable and, therefore, no surprise. But if three days go by and you know it can't be day five, then it has to be day four and that's not a surprise either.

I think I kept trying to talk to her about something meaningful but I kept yammering about stuff like this. I could focus on the headstone and the ground but couldn't bring myself to believe my mother was buried here.

I didn't cry. After a while, I just started to feel cold. I drove home and went to bed. In the morning I went to school.

"They're waiting for me. I should go."

"Do you think you should go to Alaska?"

"Yes. If Lilly and Dad want that, I do too."

"Running away?"

"Sure, why not."

"Let your father drive, okay?"

"I will."

"Careful of grizzlies."

"That too."

"What colour did you say my aura was?"

"What aura?"

CHAPTER TWENTY-TWO

Junk

Herodotus is sometimes referred to as the father of history, which is a pretty grandiose label for anyone, even a Greek. He was probably a believer that if we could understand the past, we could understand the present. Not all of us buy into this theory. I might argue that we only understand the present by understanding the present, but that sounds a heck of a lot like circular reasoning or maybe no reasoning at all. Being Greek means that he must have eaten a lot of olives. Olives, like water, can make you smart, or at least inquisitive.

When you chew those black olives with the pits, you always have to be careful not to break a tooth by chomping right into it so you swirl it around in your mouth and after you've swallowed the meat of the olive, you study the seed with your tongue. All this is very meditative and probably gave Herodotus time to work up a plan for becoming the father of history.

He became curious, for example, about the historical reasons and origins of the so-called Greco-Persian War (499–479 BC). Remember, this is BC, so the numbers go seemingly backwards, which makes it sound like the war went backwards. Did the end come first and then did it proceed to the beginning? If you were unlucky enough to be born in 499 and then got killed in the last battle of the war, maybe you lived to be minus twenty. But I digress.

Backwards or forwards, I guess the war had been going on for a long while and at this point no one really knew why they were fighting — not the Greeks and not the Persians. It had become a sort of warring fact of life. Herodotus wanted to know what the hell all the death and destruction was all about.

Herodotus wasn't sure he could get at the truth unless he studied what he thought was all of mankind's history. So he spit out his olive seed (from which a tree would one day spring to life) and he got on with it.

Herodotus travelled and questioned and he learned what he could to make sense out of his world and his war. He took a fancy to the ancient Egyptians, who were even more ancient than his people — although, at the time, Herodotus, like us today, thought of himself as contemporary, not old in any form or fashion. The Egyptians were old — at least their pyramids and their culture were — and even though Egypt wasn't real close to Greece or Persia, Herodotus had a hunch he'd learn some pretty cool shit if he rooted around there. Death, he concluded, was the most important thing in the life of an ancient Egyptian. That's what he surmised from what he found there.

When the ancient Egyptians had parties — and boy, oh boy, those were some parties — coffins would be set on the tables to remind everyone how close at hand death really was. And, of course, they built those really sturdy pyramids to house the spirits of dead pharaohs. In those days, it seemed, you really looked forward to death as something better than life. Even if you were rich, famous, and powerful at the time.

The workers — mostly slaves who didn't wear shirts — were all eating radishes, onions, and garlic for protein to build the pyramids. There were one hundred thousand or so of them doing this in the day, while at night the aristocrats sat around at parties boozing it up and staring at coffins.

Herodotus discovered a lot about ancient Egypt but nothing about the roots of the war. He concluded there was no easy answer to why the Greeks and the Persians were at war so often and so long. But if it weren't the Greeks and the Persians, it would have been the Mesopotamians and the Hittites. If not them, the Catholics and Protestants, and so forth down through the ages. The history of humanity is the history of mankind at war with itself.

Emerso

☂ ☂ ☂

Lilly and my father had, of course, wanted a report from me about what Dave had to say, but I was feeling a little confused. As we drove on out of town, I sat in the back and used my father's business laptop to write about Herodotus and the ancient Egyptians, who had been a lot on my mind lately. I knew it was a form of escape but I also knew that there were sorry souls out there who eagerly awaited my next installment of whatever was rattling around in my brain.

"Look at all the trees," Lilly said. "I thought all the trees had been cut down by now."

"Your mother loved trees," I heard my dad say.

"There's a mall."

"There's a cloud the shape of a hippopotamus," my father said.

"Where?"

"Up there."

Lilly turned on the radio to some pretty nasty rap music but my father didn't say a thing. He was glancing up at the sky every now and then looking for clouds the shape of other African animals. "Giraffe," he said, pointing.

"How can a cloud be shaped like a giraffe?" Lilly asked.

"Anything is possible," my father said over a lyrical complaint on the part of Eminem.

"I can't believe Bob Dylan is sixty-two," he said. "Martin, did you know Bob Dylan turned sixty-two?"

"He's old," I said, still thinking of the ancient Egyptians with the coffin at the party.

"Can I use your cellphone to check my e-mail?"

"Sure."

I uploaded my Herodotus piece onto my website, did a quick check for e-mail — the e-mail I never answered. I was there long enough to realize that many of those wackos who had logged onto Emerso yesterday had gone out into the world today expecting extraordinary things and found just that. I made a mental note that I would say not one more word about that exercise on Emerso.com. No explanations, no insight whatsoever. I planted a seed and walked away from it. Whatever was growing was on its own. I hoped that good would come of it.

"Martin, you hungry?" my dad asked.

"Famished," I said. I felt like I'd been dragging enormous chunks of rock uphill all day. I did a quick check of my personal e-mail and clicked on a message from Darrell.

"Dude, I've completely busted through the Gates. I have access to everything. You wouldn't believe what it's like inside. Where are you?"

I fired back, "Egg — Once the shell is cracked, it could shatter altogether. Then the yolk will be on you. Avoid open windows and other signs of danger. Don't do anything stupid."

We bought takeout Chinese and drove down a long gravel road towards a park that had campsites. My father parked near a river under a canopy of tall trees. "Hemlock," my father called them, which made me think of Socrates.

Sitting at the picnic table, eating cold Chinese take-out, we listened to the sound of the river.

"It sounds like traffic," Lilly said.

"My friend Carl, at work, he has this little machine that he turns on — just a chip in it, I guess — that sounds like a river. Just like this. He clicks it and it sounds like waves or sometimes what he calls white noise. He says it relaxes him."

"But this is real," I said. "This seems like the most real thing that's ever happened to me."

"What does that mean?" Lilly asked, touching her tongue with her finger. "Dammit." Then she popped the pin out of her tongue, stared angrily at it and threw it into the river. "Well, that was a waste of fifty dollars."

My father said nothing.

"Are we really going to Alaska?" I asked.

"See those birch trees on the other side of the river?" my father asked. "Look past them. See."

There was an adult deer and two young ones grazing in a meadow.

"Just like the Discovery Channel," Lilly said.

"Only more real," I added.

I walked to the river and put my hand into the cold, clear water. I thought about the water coming down from the mountains far away. I thought about me with my hand in the moving water, allowing the cold to numb my fingers, and then I splashed some onto my face and it made me feel like I was suddenly awake, maybe truly awake for the first time in a long while.

CHAPTER TWENTY-THREE

"Claire and I fell in love in university," my father said. "American history class. Why we had both signed up for American history, I don't know. It wasn't a required course. The professor was lazy. He made us all give presentations to the class."

"Like oral reports," Lilly said. "Sucks big time."

"Darrell almost threw up the time he had to do one."

"Your mother did the Battle of Gettysburg. I did Seward's Folly. The U.S. bought Alaska from the Russians for cash — 7.2 million dollars. In 1867. Then they discovered gold in 1869."

"I bet the Russians were pissed," Lilly said, putting a finger to her tongue.

"I fell in love with Claire while she was talking about the Battle of Gettysburg. It was one of the bloodiest battles of the American Civil War. I almost flunked the course. I didn't pay attention to anything in the class after that."

"Did you ask her out? After the Gettysburg thing?"

"No. I wrote her a poem."

"No way," Lilly said.

"It seemed like the thing to do at the time. It wasn't a good poem but it was honest."

"What did it say?"

"I don't remember."

Birds in the trees. Not a sound of civilization.

"It's like we're not on the same planet anymore. I don't know how to deal with all this... this nature thing. I mean I like it, I just don't know what to do with it. I'm going to call Wanda." Lilly retreated to the cellphone in the van.

My dad was staring at the river. "I wanted to trade places with her. I made myself believe I could do it. I wanted to be the one who was sick."

Alone with my father talking about Mom, I felt like I was trapped. I wanted to run away.

"I should have been there at the end," he said.

"No one knew when she was going to leave."

"I was discussing frozen yogurt. I was with Carl Blinn. We were coming up with adjectives to describe the texture. Then the phone rang."

I was vaguely aware of the sound of my sister's voice on the phone in the van. She wasn't talking to Wanda.

179

She was talking to Jake and she was crying. My father was breathing in a slow, halting way, rubbing his hand across the day-old stubble on his chin.

The sun was beginning to set across the river. The deer had fled from the open spaces to the safety of the deeper forest. A lone tree in the middle of the field was in the line of sight between the setting sun and me. It suddenly seemed to be on fire with the light. The light shone through the branches and created a massive corona above the canopy of the tree.

Abruptly, I had this irrational notion that my mother was not dead. I believed she was alive. She wasn't here with us in the forest but she was home. We would drive there and she would be in her studio painting a landscape where everything possessed an inner light. I felt the truth of this idea and wanted to speak it but as soon as I tried to open my mouth I felt overcome with an anger and rage that I had never, ever felt before in my life.

The sound that came out of my mouth just then was not a word. It was something primitive, something raw and horrible and very, very real to me.

Even as my father turned to look at me, I stood up and began to run — away from the river. Into the forest. My father was shouting my name and he ran after me, but I was running as fast as I possibly could, as if my life depended on it.

I ran headlong through the branches, the undergrowth. I didn't trip. My legs were not attached to the rest of me. They worked of their own doing. I felt the thin branches lash my face and I tore through thorny vines that drew blood from my cheek. And the blood tasted salty and good.

My vision blurred and my lungs began to burn but I plunged ahead. The only sound was the pounding in my ears and the deep gasping for air as I pushed my lungs to their limits.

I don't know how long I ran. My father could not keep up. When I stopped and fell to my knees, gasping for oxygen, I was alone. He was nowhere near. The evening light sifted through the forest, turned massive tree trunks to copper and gold. Before me was a forest floor with knee-high ferns — green, half unfurled, delicate.

I would rest and then I would run on. I was running to Alaska. I didn't care how far away it was or if I was going in the right direction. I could do it. I could run away and that would save me from remembering.

All I needed was enough air to fill my lungs and enough courage to get up off my knees and make my leg muscles work. I was vaguely aware of what was going on in my head. The firewalls were coming down. The places I had denied myself access to were opening up. I would muster my strength and rebuild.

I looked at the world in front of me. The trees. The light. The ferns. And realized I was in one of my mother's paintings.

Maybe I didn't need to keep running. Here was a place I could hide out. I could live here. I did not need shelter or food. I could survive on what I had in this perfect visual feast where I was not alone, because she was here. This was a place she had created. For me.

I remembered that day, when my father answered the phone. I was aware of his voice on the other end of the line. Someone was talking to him and it shocked me to the root of my being that it was my voice. I was speaking on the phone to my father from the hospital room and telling him that my mother had just died.

That day had begun like dozens before. I woke up and felt a heavy weight over top of me. Lilly stormed out of the bathroom, angry about something from her long list of things to be angry about. I could hear her throwing things in her room.

Downstairs, my father was hunched over his bowl of corn flakes in the kitchen. "I've got this damn meeting with Carl. Deadline is today. I can't go to see her until later this afternoon. Martin, I'll call the school and tell them you need to visit your mother in the hospital.

It won't hurt if you miss half a day. I'd rather send you. Lilly is acting kinda... well, you know."

"Dad, I can't go. I got that test in geometry. I've studied. I don't want to do a make-up."

He sighed. "Sure. It'll be okay. I'll call your mom. I'll tell her I'll be in later. Maybe you can drop by there after school."

"I will."

The sound of Lilly throwing a book at a wall. Traffic on the street. I had no test in math.

Lilly went out the door without eating or speaking. My father made a quick stab at the watch on his wrist with a finger and then a small storm of activity involving a briefcase, a suit jacket, the corn flake box knocked onto the floor, irrational scattering of junk off the counter looking for keys, and a final download of coffee from a cup.

"Be good, Martin," was his anthem as he walked out the door and down the sidewalk to the van.

There may have been a previous time in my life that I was not good, but it was not in the communal family memory. Although the world considered me odd, I was not prone to getting into any sort of trouble. I was not cruel; I was not belligerent. A little weird — but it came with the gender and age.

I had refused an easy out from school to visit my mother in the hospital. She'd been there for two months now. She would not get better. I found each visit more painful than the one before.

Outside, I felt the weight of the morning more intense than before. The sky was heavy with dark grey clouds and, as I walked down the driveway, I felt as if I was holding up the sky. It was sitting on my shoulders. I was hoping Mr. Miller would play his guitar in math today. I was praying that Kathy would talk to me. I didn't care if she talked about her crush on Kyle or if she told me how cute Rob Dobson was. I just hoped she would talk to me.

I found myself looking at the flowers in people's yards as I walked along, naming them in my head: marigold, pansy, shasta daisy, calendula. Cosmos. But the walking was not easy. I was the 75,000-kilo kid. I tried to do complicated three-digit multiplication in my head to keep focused: 267 times 976 equals what?

It was the fire drill during third period that sent us out into the light drizzle. My hair collected the droplets of water. Everyone complained they were getting wet. When the bell rang for us to go back in I told Darrell I had to leave.

"Where you gonna go?"

"I don't know," I said.

"I'll come with you."

"No. Thanks."

"Here's a couple of bucks for the bus."

"How'd you know I wanted to take a bus?"

Darrell shrugged. "Take it."

I didn't have a cent on me. I took the money and turned to go. Mr. Miller was watching me as I walked away but he didn't say anything.

The nurse left the room after checking the tubes in my mom's arm. I was thinking that I hated hospitals, that if you had to be sick, you should be in a place that looked completely different from this.

She was not looking good. She had a lifeless colour to her skin, a little less light in the eyes. The sky sat on the roof of the hospital and the only thing keeping the building from collapsing was me.

"Don't look so glum," she said.

"Some days I'm a little moody," I answered.

"You've always been such a serious boy." The hint of a smile seemed to cost her.

"Dad'll be here this afternoon."

"He works too hard."

"His job sucks."

"He should have been a poet."

"Right."

"I miss being outside. How are my flowers?"

"Going crazy. It's like a jungle." Realizing I had forgotten to water them and they would be dying. Hoping it would rain big-time today and coax them back to life. "I'll weed them this weekend."

"Leave the dandelions."

"And I'll try not to disturb the snails."

"I lie here and my brain gets caught up in a circle of foolish things that go round and round and I can't seem to stop it. It's not even anything important. I think about a painting that I want to finish. I worry about your father not living up to his creative potential. I worry about Lilly. Did she ditch Jake yet?"

"Not yet. But any day now."

"And you, Martin."

"You don't need to worry about me."

"It's you I worry about the most," she said.

When she held out her hand to me, I could see the pain in her face. She was tugging at me, pulling me towards her, and some part of me was resisting. But I gave in. I leaned forward, and I allowed her to pull my head to her chest. She ran her fingers through my hair, which was still damp from the drizzle outside.

She seemed impossibly fragile. I closed my eyes, wished I could find a voice for the love I felt for her, but it was drowned out by fear.

I did not move for what seemed like a long, long while. I concentrated on the light pressure of my mother's fingers on my neck and the back of my head. Then I felt her grip diminish, and when her hands fell away her eyes were closed and she had fallen asleep.

I sat back down in the chair by the bed and watched her face, which now seemed free of pain. She was breathing a shallow, steady rhythm, and I looked up at the blank TV screen on the far wall. I could see a reflection of the two of us in it. A son and his mother in a hospital room. The reflection in the dark glass seemed like a portal into another place — a stark, two-dimensional world without colour or energy.

The nurse came into the room shortly after that to check on my mother. She left abruptly, but I did not seem to understand the reason. She returned with a doctor and another nurse and I was ushered out of the room. It was as if it was happening to someone else — the boy reflected in the dark TV screen above — because that's the image I focused on until I was led out of the room.

I sat in a chair in a waiting room and no one talked to me. Then I was allowed to go back into the room with my mother. It was then that I made the phone call to my father. The doctor asked me for the number and said he would call, but I said no. And I called him. Then I called the school and told Mr. Cohen to get Lilly out of class.

I didn't look at my mom even though she was right there in the room with me. The doctor and nurse were talking to me, but I didn't understand the meaning of words spilling out of their mouths.

And then I felt the great weight that had been upon my shoulders disappear. I felt much lighter. I straightened my back and sat upright in the chair, looking out at the rain. Aside from that, I didn't feel much of anything. And that was the way I stayed for a long time.

CHAPTER TWENTY-FOUR

I was kneeling in the forest. My hands were clenched — two fists full of dirt and pine needles from the forest floor. I heard a mosquito buzz near my ear, and then it landed on my cheek. I felt the small sharp pain of it piercing and drawing blood from me.

Then I heard someone running towards me. Lilly.

"Martin." She nearly collapsed beside me. She touched my face, then looked at the blood on her finger. "Jesus, Martin."

"What am I going to do now?"

"I don't know."

I threw the dirt in my fists. Not at Lilly. At nothing. I felt the anger well up inside me. "Why did she have to die?"

"We better find Dad. I followed him after you ran off. Then we split up. You scared him pretty bad."

"I don't care. I was there with her when she died."

"We know that. You called Dad, remember?"

"Now I do."

It was almost dark by the time we found our way to the gravel road and met up with my father. I'd never seen him look so scared. He pulled me to him and held on tightly. He didn't ask me to explain. I could remember what she looked like now. I could see her face very clearly in my mind. I could remember what she looked like when she was healthy — fussing with her flowers in the back yard. And I could remember her in the hospital — I could see the pain; I could see what it was like to die. And the rage that accompanied those images was so great, I was afraid to speak.

When we arrived at the van, the side door was open and it was full of mosquitoes.

"We're not going to Alaska, are we?" Lilly asked.

"I don't think so," my father said. "Let's go get a pizza somewhere and then find a motel."

I sat down in the back seat of the van. My father started the engine and we drove back the way we had come in. I realized in my silence how angry I was at him for changing his mind. The forest around us was dark and silent.

"I'm getting back together with Jake," Lilly said.

"He said he made a mistake. Jake is like the best thing that ever happened to me."

I bit my thumb until it bled.

Opinions/Advice/Stuff/Junk/Meaning of Life: You Choose

Language limits what we know and what we think. Language is limited and our minds are limited by it. What one generation "understands" to be true, the next generation discovers to be false — because people change, times change, ideas change. Language changes. Truth is probably unknowable, and so we fumble with half-truths.

History is shaped more by misunderstanding than understanding, more by mystery than fact. Some philosophers I think try to deal with this. The German Jewish philosopher Ludwig Wittgenstein was one of those men. He was a teacher who told his students something like this: "I want to be able to move you away from something that is disguised nonsense to something that is obvious nonsense." Better to know something is false (even if you continue to live by it) than to believe something is true when it is actually untrue.

Wittgenstein admitted to having a "low misery threshold," which made him a pretty unhappy character at Cambridge, where he hung out with the likes of Bertrand Russell. Ludwig projected some of his unhappiness in a philosophical way by getting into arguments about the nature of reality and how we perceive it. In one classic case, during a *tête à tête* among masters, he adamantly refused to believe that there was not a rhinoceroses under his desk. He did not assert there was a rhinoceros there, just that no one could absolutely prove otherwise.

Wittgenstein became a soldier during the First World War and helped save a fellow soldier who was wounded on the battlefield. He learned to believe in the ultimate reality of pain and suffering, but everything else was up for debate.

Born in 1889, Wittgenstein died in 1951, the year of the first colour television broadcast in the United States. Wittgenstein viewed himself as a kind of therapist for misunderstanding. He hoped philosophy could cure you of all the screwed up ideas stuck in your head that rule your life. This did not always go over well at parties and more often than not, almost no one (other than Bertrand Russell, maybe) knew what the hell he was talking about.

Wittgenstein did succeed in distancing himself from his own misery by writing cumbersome, hard-to-read books with titles like *Tractates Logico-Philosophicus*, which would make a great name for a rap group if anyone wants to borrow it.

Like other intellectuals and writers before him, Ludwig W. used his ideas to escape from the hard work of living with himself. But like Mick Jagger once said, "It's all right letting yourself go, as long as you can get yourself back."

Emerso

🌢 🌢 🌢

"Who exactly are you angry at?" Dave asked.

"Everyone. Everything."

"Could you begin to narrow that down?"

"I'm really pissed off at you, for starters."

"Why me?"

"I was okay the way I was. I didn't necessarily like who I was but I could live with it. I'm not sure I can live with this."

"You never told me about being in the room when she died."

"Everyone knew I was there. I called my father while I was standing beside her bed. It wasn't exactly a secret."

"But you had shut it out of your mind."

"I kept it in a box."

"And now the box is open?"

"And I'm not sure I can stand it."

"A lot of people have to learn to live with pain, with truth. Join the club."

"This is all you have to offer now that I'm acting the way everyone wanted me to act? I hate all of you for doing this to me."

"You can hate me if you want. Just don't cut me out. Gotta keep coming here. Gotta keep talking."

"I don't feel like being nice to anyone anymore. No more good deeds. What are they all going to make of me at school?"

"You're probably going to piss a lot of people off."

"That's what I'm hoping for."

"How'd you learn to drive, anyway?"

"I just figured it out, I guess."

"Better stay off the road. The world doesn't need another angry driver."

"I could be good at road rage."

"You going to go back to the cemetery, though?"

"I can't."

"You should. Sometime when you're ready."

"When will that be?"

"I don't know," Dave said.

"That's all you can say? Maybe you are right for having those self-doubts. Maybe you're not very good at your job. Look at me. I was better off before I started coming here. What if I sued your ass for malpractice?"

"I don't know. If you feel you have to do it, then go for it."

After a while it felt like we were talking in circles. I wanted to hit something or break something and I had this feeling that if I did, it would give Dave great satisfaction. He'd see it as some kind of success, so I wasn't going to give him the satisfaction.

CHAPTER TWENTY-FIVE

Gloom was the persistent mood as we pulled back up into the driveway. "Welcome to Mt. McKinley," I said out loud. "Mt. McKinley is the highest mountain in Alaska, in North America for that matter. It's 20,320 feet, to be precise."

And I was going to have to climb that damn mountain day after day from now on. With the overwhelming weight of the sky settling down on my shoulders again, I would have to attempt to climb those forbidding icy slopes.

"We're home," my dad said.

"I'm gonna go call Jake," Lilly said and walked into the house.

"Why would she want to hang onto Jake?" I asked him.

"Lilly needs something to hang onto. We all do."

"Understatement of the century."

"Martin, we're going to make it."

"I don't know."

"I'm quitting my job. I hate it. I hate it even more because Claire would hate the fact I stayed with it."

"What are you going to do, write poetry? Now there would be a brilliant career move." It felt natural now to be giving my father a hard time.

"Yeah, I am. First I'm gong to get out all of your mother's paintings. I'm going to photograph them outside in natural light. This is something I told her I would do but never did."

I wanted to tell him about the paintings — the scanned images of the paintings I'd posted on Emerso — but I didn't. He didn't know about the website. I still didn't want him to know. I wanted that to remain my own secret kingdom — this fantasy world inhabited by me and those other freaks out there who found "my world" something they could relate to. As Emerso, I could set off shotgun epiphanies. Miracles could blossom in strangers' lives just because I said it should be so.

But no one was going to be able to create a miracle for me.

"I'll freelance," my dad said. "I'll do some advertising work but just enough to scrape by. We'll live on the cheap but I'll work from home. What do you think?"

"You know what we called you, Lilly and me?"

"The Invisible Man," he said.

I suddenly felt guilty.

"I may have been invisible but I wasn't deaf. And by the way, I hate golf. If I ever turn on the Golf Channel again, destroy the television at once."

"I will," I promised, but I wasn't thinking about him, I was thinking about me and the misery that still haunted me.

"Let's do some father-son thing. What do you want to do?"

"I want to clean up the back yard," I said.

And that's what we did. We weeded the flower beds, cleaned up some trash, snipped some grass with hand cutters. I transplanted some small cosmos dwarfed by the older growth. I dug into the soil with my fingers and transplanted the flowers to a place they'd have more room. Then I watered them with my mom's old watering can.

"Some of them are perennials," he said. "They keep coming back every year from the root."

"Some just drop a zillion seeds and keep coming back that way. Calendula. Asters."

All night I climbed Mt. McKinley's jagged slope. It was dark, cold. The winds were horrendous. I couldn't get a good handhold and my feet kept slipping. I wanted to let go and fall.

When I woke up in the morning, my father was out in the yard with her paintings. He leaned them against trees in the morning sun and was taking pictures of them with his Pentax mounted on a tripod.

Lilly was burning pop tarts. "Jake's picking me up in a few minutes. Want a ride to school?"

"Sure," I said. My venom supply was still topped up. Why not get a good kick-start with Jake?

A car horn, three hammer blows. My father, pausing from his work, waving to Jake; Jake not responding. His eyes were straight ahead, music on loud, bobbing his head slightly, reptilian.

I got into the back seat without asking. "Dweeb transport?" was all he said to Lilly. She shrugged.

Between tracks on the CD playing I asked Jake how long he'd had that zit on the back of his neck. "You know," I said, "the one that looks like Vesuvius ready to erupt?"

Lilly turned and gave me a look of shock. Jake was raising his hand to give me the finger, eyes in the rearview mirror. I beat him to the draw.

I was surprised that I didn't feel any satisfaction in this. I wanted so bad to be nasty but this was just kid's stuff. Jake was an easy target. He was Pearl Harbor and I had all the planes. But I couldn't seem to drop the load.

"No more mister nice guy," was all Jake said to me when I climbed out at school. I didn't thank him for the ride. Lilly grabbed me before I walked away. I thought she was going to yell at me. Instead, she shoved her school schedule in my hand. "You need me, you'll know how to find me," she said. I walked towards school. It didn't look anything like the same place I'd left yesterday.

After a major fire burns through an old growth forest, after the fire has seemingly run its course and the fire fighters are all home washing the soot out of their clothes and staring at their singed eyelashes in the mirror, sometimes there are roots deep underground still smouldering. All they need is a little oxygen.

I think the other kids could smell something burning in the classroom during my first two periods of the day. Teachers droned and students sat droopy-eyed and uninterested. I stared at the back of Kathy Bringhurst. I liked her hair and that surprised me. I had to admit to myself that I liked the way her hair looked. It was long and brown and kind of straight. It was nothing Hollywood gorgeous, just real girl hair and I liked looking at it.

And I was totally shocked. Shocked because I was one hundred percent sure I hated everything in this world. There was not one thing right about what was going on in the universe and it was as if everything that happened was some kind of punishment for me.

Except for this. I liked her hair.

The bell rang. I couldn't even tell you what the teacher had been talking about for the last fifty minutes, but the blackboard was full of ambitious words and diagrams. Apparently it had been an English class and Ms. Wallace was talking about a poem by Walt Whitman.

I caught up to her outside class. "Kathy."

"Martin, I didn't even see you in class."

"Invisibility runs in my family."

"I didn't mean it that way."

"How are you?" I asked.

She had that sadness still about her. Scott Rutledge was still dead. He had not come back to life as she had hoped. Her dreams were shattered. Her heart broken and scattered to the highways headed off in all directions. "I'm doing better," she said.

"I really like your hair."

"Thanks. I was thinking of getting it cut."

"No," I said. "Please don't."

She didn't understand, I know. And I'm sure I appeared more the freak than usual. I had discovered one blessed thing in the world I liked — only one thing. And she was considering cutting it off. She studied the weirdness in my face. "Okay. I won't cut it."

My soul dredged up from the sewers of Hades.

"Maybe I'll trim the split ends."

"Sure," I said as if giving permission. "You can do that. Walk you to math?"

Math had been on a major downhill skid ever since the HMMWMT had exhibited dementia during class. Whatever was going on in class was as exciting as last year's lint. The new guy, Mr. Templeton, didn't seem to care. He droned and droned and then gave an overly ambitious homework assignment that no one would be able to finish. I stationed myself in the back of the room so I could stare at the back of Kathy some more but I decided not to talk to her again because whatever was going to come out of my mouth would probably sound fully flaked.

Darrell made first contact with me at lunch. I hadn't seen him all morning and at lunch he wanted to know where I had disappeared to yesterday. The Egg Man had thought to bring an extra sandwich for me in cele-bration of his own success. I warned him I was feeling a little testy, that if I said anything rude, he should chalk it up to simple psychosis.

"Emerso, I had my way with Microsoft."

"The challenge of a lifetime, right?"

"You bet. I hacked past all the firewalls and all kinds of stuff only Bill Gates himself could have dreamed up. I was there. I was inside the corp. Adrenalin rush or what? Access to everything. Financials, R&D, Bill Gates' personal hobby files — some weird shit there. Company memos. Short range, long-term planning, info on corporate spying. You name it."

"Once again, hearty congratulations. And then you got arrested?"

"No. I was tricked." But Darrell was still smiling. "I was suckered in and it was beautiful."

"I don't get it."

"Hackers' heaven. I thought I'd busted down the doors just like I'd always dreamed, but it was a virtual space — a virtual version of Microsoft. I was lured right in like a skunk headed for some smelly mackerel in a Havaheart trap. It was all fake, perfectly and convincingly so."

"How did you figure that out?"

"I didn't. I back out of the whole shebang, I cover my tracks, I bask in the glory of it all, and then I get this e-mail marked urgent. They offered me a job."

Deep down, Darrell was still the eight-year-old nerd who had long ago been my best friend when we used to perform smelly experiments or put obnoxious concoctions on the road for cars to run over. He had more to tell but I was annoyed that he thought this so important. Little boy games. I took a bite out of the sandwich he had brought. Classic Darrell egg salad with paprika. I added that to my list of things I didn't hate about the world. So far it was a small list of two items.

"Why did they offer you a job?"

"Only a handful of hackers — five to be exact — have ever gotten that far into Microsoft. The virtual site was set up to deceive hackers into thinking they we were in. But it was set up so that only the best of the best could succeed. And if you are that good, they want you on their team. Or at least they want your brain."

"Did you tell them it was a package deal, they can't have your brain without your body attached?"

"We haven't gotten that far with our negotiations. But it's looking like great things are ahead. *Salut.*"

We bumped egg salad sandwiches.

Chapter Twenty-Six

☂ ☂ ☂

(New heading) Self-Definition

We are memory; we are emotions. We are each worth about ninety-seven cents if reduced to our basic chemicals. It used to be sixty-two cents but the price of everything has gone up. If we dwell on our own insignificance then I suppose everything could seem pretty pointless but I'm not about to tell you that here. We all come into the world more or less the same. And the end of everyone's story is the pretty much the same.

We are not much more than bugs smashed on the windshield of life — don't think that is profound or anything because I'm borrowing from that Mark Knopfler song.

You think you have problems, I think I have problems. But take a scoop of any history and you'll discover that it mostly comes up turds. If my memory serves me well (and it does), I could tell you that Galveston, Texas had a hurricane in 1900 and six thousand people drowned.

That was the same year Sigmund Freud published his book *Interpretation of Dreams*. Extrapolate that on your Texas Instrument. The next year Queen Victoria died, which may be seen by some as a blessing — not so much because of her but what she represented. She had no choice in who she was because of the blood she was born with. In her name, the English terrorized anyone who was not English — barbarism in the name of civilization, that sort of thing. (An old sad song, a wailing.)

President McKinley was assassinated that year and later someone named a mountain in Alaska after him. (Alaska had been bought at a kind of yard sale of real estate from the Russians for spare change in 1867.) McKinley's assassin, Leon Colugos, had Russian blood in him and he claimed to be an anarchist — a guy who doesn't believe in anything organized. In reality, he was not much different from the American soldiers or the British riflemen who all agreed it was okay to kill a person who represented something you didn't approve of. Nobody named a mountain after Colugos, not even the Society of American Anarchists who had a hard time agreeing on anything except that no government is good government.

This history lesson is not in vain, however. I just want to point out that we are gum on a shoe, you and I as individuals. If you don't think this is important, go watch a rerun of *Beverly Hills 90210,* or better yet, read Dostoyevsky's *The Idiot.* Boy, that would cheer you up.

So I'm on a rant. Enjoy it or bug out of the zone. Where was I? Up to 1902. You get gramophone recordings of people like Enrico Caruso who sang opera. A bunch of silly little wars, tribal battles, nothing global to really get your gobs into. Just infighting, small civil wars, attempts at revolution, mudslides on villages, viruses, smallpox, religious persecution, and so forth. Your average year.

1903 is kind of interesting, though, because Wilbur and Orville (fine names for cartoon characters) Wright put themselves aloft on a machine from those sand dunes down at Kitty Hawk, North Carolina. Technology would continue to improve and commercial airlines would one day flush the contents of their toilets outside while flying over your town and people would wonder about these odd little summer showers. 1903 was also the year Henry Ford started his company and a million or so people down though the years would have incredibly boring jobs working on assembly lines. Those assembly lines switched over from Model A's to tanks and other military vehicles when the big wars heated up a few years later.

The Russians and the Japanese were killing each other over who owned Korea in 1904. The Russians went nuts in 1905 and there was lots of blood in the streets, people trampled by horses, mutiny on the *Potemkin* like in that old black and white film they showed you in school, baby carriages rolling down steps while soldiers shot weapons. Screaming mothers. And so forth.

San Francisco had an earthquake in 1906 followed by a fire that pretty well burned the city down, but only 500 people died, not like in 1908 when an earthquake in southern Italy killed 150,000. (Notice I skipped 1907 where the usual run of bad luck happened but memory fails me except to note there was a "financial panic" where only a handful of rich cats lost fur and jumped to their deaths from buildings. It wasn't quite the human freefall of 1929 but a kind of dry run, so to speak.)

I'm going to try to end this decade on an upbeat note and remind you that Robert Peary made it to the North Pole in 1909 and discovered to everyone's amazement that it was cold and that there was no Santa Claus. And in 1910 the Boy Scouts of America was incorporated and nearly a century later, Boy Scouts would still be asking their mothers to sew "Personal Hygiene" merit badges onto their uniforms.

That's my random decade. My hope is that it cheers you up somewhat in thinking that your own little moans and groans (you didn't get the Play Station for Christmas, your investment in HDTV didn't double your money, your dreams of becoming a skeletal fashion model were crushed by the girth of your thighs — etc., etc.) don't amount to a hill of beans in this world, to paraphrase Humphrey Bogart, who probably didn't even realize that smoking was bad for his health at that point in his life and so he could actually enjoy a cigarette without guilt.

If you are still with me, you realize that a kind of grey pall hangs over the Emerso.com site today. It's an attempt to weed out the mere passersby on this potholed information highway, to discourage those who are not totally loyal to the cause — the mere hitchhikers and hangabouts. In an effort to streamline and serve our target audience, we want to weed out anyone who is not hard-core.

And for those hard-core, hard-ass fans still with me (and I know you are there even though I will never, ever answer fan mail), I should leave you with brief reports about what happened right after the North Pole and Boy Scouts. Once again, there was the usual run of bloodbaths, headlopping, and death by fungus on all continents. Also, in 1911, aircraft were first used as a military weapons in the Turkish-Italian War, which you may not have ever heard of unless you were a Turk or an Italian. A lot of people died in China bringing about a revolution that ended the Manchu dynasty, but then Chinese emperors were not exactly legendary for their kindness to peasants and blood was just waiting to be spilled. Mexico had a revolution. Fires in factories were big that year (I almost said "hot"), a notable one being at the Triangle Shirtwaist Company in New York where 145 workers were killed. A few were Italian immigrants who had survived the earthquake of 1908.

After that, it's pretty much a gruesome road leading to WWI. It starts off with a whole lot of cruelty and suffering that takes place in small wars involving Bulgaria, Greece, Serbia, Turkey, and Romania. This is 1912 I'm talking about, quite the year for tragedy if you toss into the mix the *Titanic* sinking and fifteen hundred drowning because they didn't have enough lifeboats. But you knew about that one because you saw the movie, and the upside is that near the tail-end of the century investors in the movie would make scads and scads of money. Yahoo.

But that's another website.

Emerso

CHAPTER TWENTY-SEVEN

The question driving the blinding confusion that was in my brain had no easy answer. I spent hours at my keyboard writing rants about anything I could get into my head. The destruction of the codfish in the North Atlantic, the decline of the right whales, the barefaced bozo-ness of restarting the arms race with new missiles in space, genetically modified foods, drug companies more interested in profits than cures for disease.

I had stopped showing off what I knew about existentialism and German philosophers. I could tell from the postings on the bulletin board and the e-mails I would not answer that my old clientele was drifting away. I was down to cynics, hard heads, hard-asses, hard cases. My kind of people.

Thanks to Darrell's ultra-clever web mastering, my site drew spiders and forged automatic links. Punch in "revolution" or "anarchy" at Google and you'd end up with Emerso.com as maybe number three on your list. Some of my tribe were fascists; some were disenfranchised down-and-out homeless people tapping into my head-space from the computer in the downtown public library.

I forged diatribes about the meaninglessness of the universe and the corruption of the human spirit; I denounced right-wingers, and when I grew weary of that, I denounced left-wingers. I despised the status quo in such eloquent terms that I drew kudos from weirdos who claimed to be making bombs in their basements.

My hatred of humanity, I argued, was based on my love of humanity. I raged because I wanted to change the world as it so pitifully existed. My website was my lever and the web itself was the fulcrum. I don't know what strange alien turf I was standing on, but I was still trying to lift a gargantuan weight. And I was trying to do it with words.

My father, on the other hand, had become enamoured with food and cooking. Our kitchen was crowded with cans and boxes of unusual and exotic forms of sustenance. The refrigerator was stuffed with organic vegetables. I was not opposed to eating what he cooked. Lilly made faces and stuck out her pierced and baubled tongue but she ate what he prepared nonetheless.

I liked the way our house smelled when he made his own spaghetti sauce. That was not the case at first. But the wafting aroma of tomato, garlic, oregano, cumin, and all the rest was something I grew to appreciate. It was number three on my list of the things I liked about the world. It was still a small but growing list and I'd averaged one likeable new thing per week. But it was not enough to sustain me. The anger was not going away.

I sucked it in during school. I concentrated on invisibility, positioned myself behind Kathy. Looked at her hair. But began to realize this was getting pretty looped.

Corporate scalpers heard about Darrell from a mole inside Microsoft and he had a few other job offers. No one knew yet he was only fifteen and a kid who had received a modest C+ in health class. Darrell claimed that his mind wandered and he just wasn't interested in the human reproductive system.

Every once in a while I broke my own rules and actually read the e-mail people sent to my site. I was beginning to think that Emerso.com was headed into its final days. I was attracting too many weird fans. Mostly embittered people like me trying desperately to find someone to blame. Not long ago, people would write asking me for advice (even though I never, ever answered their mail) and they would imagine I was responding to them personally when they read my postings — say, my short thesis on Darwinism and deism —

and then assume it was a pretty good answer to a personal query about what to do about a husband who ignores his wife in favour of fixing his '57 Chevy.

But now that I was attracting the let's-make-bombs-in-our-basement crowd, I was being asked if I wanted to join a neo-Nazi party or an organization called ICHTHOS that wanted to free the fish from all the world's aquariums. I was asked to be a spokesperson for better living conditions for chickens about to be slaughtered for KFC. A fringe political bunch called the Blue Party wanted to know if I would run in a federal election. One woman in an unnamed correctional institution asked me if I would marry her and father her child. And so forth.

I would have to talk to Darrell about pulling the plug on Emerso and we'd have to do a pretty clean wipe. I don't think I'd want it wandering around cyberspace as some websites have been known to do — like a commercial fishermen's plastic filament driftnet cut loose and travelling with the currents causing endless death and destruction to thousands of fish for God knows how long.

The thought of cutting myself off from my Emerso persona, however, gave me another pang. I had set myself up as some kind of surrogate parent to a family — a bizarre assortment of humanity for sure, people I'd be afraid to be in the same room with. But a family nonetheless. My own crippled real family was one thing but I needed more. And if I cut off Emerso, it might be like lopping off my right foot to save me from the gangrene that would seep into the rest of my body and kill me. It was going to hurt like hell.

I scrolled through the pithy, the posturing, and the paranoia-filled e-mails until I came to this one:

"What is Emerso angry about?" was the entire contents of the unsigned message that came from the address axletwister@hotmail.com.

Screw you, I responded in my head, but my fingers would not tap the keys.

I scrolled on to other messages. Some idiot had downloaded the entire contents of *Mein Kampf* and sent it to me as an attachment. One I would not open.

Another marriage proposal. This one was from a seventy-year-old woman in a nursing home who claimed to be political prisoner.

And then this one came yet again, but in a more personal form.

"What is Martin angry about?" It came from the same source as the earlier anger question.

Only two real options, I figured: Dave or Darrell. Either one, messing with my head. I phoned Dave first. He said he was between clients.

"Not me. Someone else has found you out. What were they asking?"

"Nothing important."

"How are you doing? You skipped your last appointment."

"Things are working out. I'm cured, maybe."

"Doesn't work like that. 'Here, kid. Take a pill. Fix your head.'"

"How come I didn't get the machine?" I asked. "I always get your machine." Dave's message was always the same. Dave's voice: "Hi, you've reached the machine. Leave a message after the bleep." He called it a bleep.

"I'm going to take some time off. A kind of sabbatical. I've got some travelling I want to do. I'm referring my clients on to other professionals. One by one."

"Then?"

"I'll do a disappearing act."

"You bastard. You're running away."

"I think of it as running *to*."

I felt rage. "I should never have trusted you in the first place."

"Martin, I'm not leaving until you say it's okay to leave."

"Like I said, I'm cured."

"Convince me. Come over some time. We'll talk."

"Nah. That's okay. Just refer me on to someone else."

"I don't want to do that."

"Why not?"

"Because you and I are a lot alike."

Darrell swore that he had not sent me the e-mail questions either. It was somebody else. I read the origin of the mail to him over the phone.

"I can trace it. A little program I borrowed while snooping around. Stay on the line."

I scrolled backward through old messages on my screen from a while back. I had almost forgotten about my promo package predicting extraordinary things in the lives of my good followers. Guys had made up with girlfriends, a couple of UFO stories, religious experiences, someone remembered a past life while eating frozen yogurt, nobody reported anything negative — all good . stuff, some of it pretty boring, but my old fans were impressed. Emerso had set off scads of small miracles.

And then Emerso had changed. Hard-core, hard-ass. A more comfortable identity in some ways. I liked to rant, to vent, to extrapolate new cynical meanings from history. The new-age flakes had no doubt moved on to loftier sites than mine. Now it was just me, the fascists, and the committee to prevent penguins from being exposed to television.

"Got an answer for you, Martini," Darrell said.

"You're good."

"No, Martin, I'm bad. Bad is good in this biz."

"So who is it?"

"Kensington Miller."

"Heavy Metal Math."

"Whodathunkit?" One of Darrell's favourite expressions from when we were little kids.

Chapter Twenty-Eight

It was really strange seeing Mr. Miller again. He had bags under his eyes and he was still unshaven — a beard now, partly grey, covered his chin. He tugged at it as he looked at me.

"Martin."

"Mr. Miller, it's been a while."

He shrugged. "I'm into this new lifestyle thing."

He opened the door wider and I walked in. His new lifestyle was pretty much like the one Lilly and Darrell and I had encountered before. It involved closed blinds and a cornucopia of multi-coloured beer cans strewn about the living room, some crushed, some not. Mr. Miller flicked off the TV. Oprah faded off the tube.

"It's recycling day. I was just trying to get things organized," he said, knocking a couple of empty Moosehead beer cans off a chair for me to sit down.

"You thinking about going back to teaching?"

"Nah. I don't think they'll let me back."

"Why not try?"

"I've been kind of busy." He swept his arm round the room as if to suggest he'd been at work at something.

"How'd you know Emerso was me?"

"I didn't at first. Dave must have told me to check out the site. I was into killing time. The Internet can be a great place to go if you don't have anything you want to do."

"He promised not to tell anyone."

"He didn't tell me it was you. Hey, I didn't get it until you started to change."

"Emerso changed."

"Yeah, he got on this kick of ranting about how screwed up everything was. Then I read through every-thing — old stuff and new— and I put the pieces togeth-er. That is some education we gave you at school."

"You introduced me to the German philosophers."

"Stay away from Nietzsche, okay?"

"Now we just do math in math class."

"Sucks, doesn't it?"

"I always covered my tracks. Never said anything personal on the site. It was always Emerso."

"It was always you, kid. And I know the answer to my question. I know who you're angry at."

"Then why ask it?"

"I know the answer but you don't."

"This is stupid." I realized I had made a mistake coming here.

"Tell me then. Who are you angry at?"

I sucked in a breath. "I'm angry at me."

"Maybe a little," he shot back. "But that's not where the deep-down anger is coming from."

I said nothing.

Mr. Kensington Miller picked up a couple of empty beer cans and dribbled the leftover contents onto a dead fern plant. "Martin, I know. I've been there. My father died when I was fourteen. He worked construction — he built bridges for a living. My mother had been trying to get him to quit for a long while. He always said it wasn't dangerous. And the money was good. When she complained, he said that she didn't appreciate him. He said that none of us did. After his accident at work, I was angry for a long time."

"Who were you angry at?"

"I was angry at him."

My father was in the back yard when I took the keys from the kitchen table and started the van. It was the first time I'd ever driven around town in the daylight. I kept trying to tell myself that what I was feeling was wrong. Not logical. But what if Mr. Miller had been right? I felt a horrible kind of guilt for feeling the way I did. I focused on the driving. Slow and cautious. Keep the animal in the cage.

I hated the antiseptic smell of the hospital more than anything as I entered it. I took the elevator to the third floor and went to room 317, walked in. One bed was empty. In another was an old man with an oxygen tube up his nose. He was asleep.

I stood by the empty bed where my mother had died and looked up at the TV screen as I had before. I studied my muddy reflection in the dark screen, reconnecting that day with this one, reconnecting myself to that hollow image in the screen. I closed my eyes and slipped back to that time. I saw how easy it had been to make my great escape. But I knew where I had to go next.

I was shocked at how difficult it was for me to find the exact location of the grave. Everything was green. The place had just been mowed maybe a couple of days ago. As if on purpose, I was making detours in one direction and then another until I wove my way from the older headstones to the newer ones.

And as I stood there facing her grave, I felt noth-ing. I knew where I was and why I was here, but it was like I'd tricked myself into looking for a solution to my problem. And there was no solution. I felt hollowed out, like that dead image of me in the hospital TV. I did not cry.

I heard the sound of crows in the trees nearby. I leaned down and touched the headstone and it felt warm. Polished granite. Dark, in sunlight. Behind it someone had crammed in a paper coffee cup and on the ground were two cigarette butts.

Maybe it was the guy who had mowed the grass on his coffee break. Or someone who had been walking through the cemetery. They'd thought nothing of leaving their trash here.

A kind of tidal wave swept through me as I picked up the trash. I hated whoever had done this.

I tried to say something, something to her. I wanted to say that I loved her and that I wish I had said something more there in the hospital room that day and that I wish I had cried. I wanted to ask her to forgive me, but instead I whispered, "Why did you leave us?" And I placed the blame squarely on her.

But as soon as the words were out, I knew I got it all wrong. What I had known to be true, I now felt in my bones. *It wasn't her fault.*

I lay down on the grass and pulled my knees to my chest. I began to speak to her and say the things that I needed to say. Bad timing, but it was all I could do. I closed my eyes and heard the sound of the wind in the treetops. I could hear the traffic, too, but it sounded like the river in the forest.

When I opened my eyes, it took a few minutes for the world to get back into focus. Sunlight spilled through the branches and filtered through the pale green leaves so that it seemed like every tree was illuminated from within.

I realized I had done a pretty fair job of pushing away the memories I had of my mother. If I wasn't careful, it was all going to slip away and that was not what I wanted at all. Emerso and I had been very careful about the construction of a safe and cynical alternate world to inhabit. My self-appointed dictator status in that nation was about to come to an end.

When it came time to pull the plug on Emerso.com, I wanted to leave nothing there in its place except a vacuum. My fans would find other diversions, but my so-called wisdom and my many opinions would not be available.

My father was in the kitchen when I came home. He had the radio up quite loud — old music from the seventies. I think it was ABBA. He was making spaghetti sauce from scratch. Tomato and garlic and basil and something else. He hadn't even noticed the van was gone. I hung the keys up on the hook where they were supposed to be.

"Lilly's had another fight with Jake," he said. "Be nice to her, okay?"

"I'll give it a try."

"Taste this."

"Not enough garlic," I said.

"More garlic coming up," he said.

As he reached for another garlic clove, I asked him if I could read some of his poetry. He pulled down a Hilroy notebook from a kitchen shelf and handed it to me.

Darrell was exuberant about his plan to shut down Emerso.com. At twelve midnight, three days after my final posting, it would "go off the air." The domain name would cease to exist. All trace would be gone as if it had never been there. Emerso.com would disappear as mysteriously as it had emerged. I would not reveal my identity but the final words would not be mine. I decided to end the kingdom of Emerso with the disappearance of the king, an abdication of that czar of wisdom, compassion, arrogance, and ultimately dark sarcasm that had been me. But there would be no hi-tech send-off with bells and whistles as Darrell had suggested. Only one last message — the first ever e-mail to Emerso.com's visitors. And it would go to everyone who had ever visited Emerso. It was a poem written by my father, for my mother, but now a final gift to my lost tribe:

I give you the square root of sky,
the large province of hope and the view
from the top of the hill at the end of the beach.
I give you finches in the apple tree,
sunset, west over ice,
the wedge of sunlight in late afternoon
with its warm explosion of cloud
at the end of a dark day — the brooding clouds overhead
unable to repress the adventure.
I give you guardians in the form of cloud
and snow and summer rain on calendula.
I give you balance and assurance to allow
you to dance along the edge of disaster
without looking down.

Here is the compass from my past
and the map I've kept hidden in my heart —
the tools necessary to find the path
from despair to happiness.
And in the wind
you will find the solved mystery
of being and moving at once.

I give you the polished remains of glass
washed up on every shore
sculpted into gems
and all the lost toys of our childhood,

the right to reinvent any world
to fit your dreams.
I give you back all
that knowledge and responsibility has taken away
and so I set you free.

AGMV Marquis

MEMBER OF SCABRINI MEDIA

Quebec, Canada
2004